DRY-GULCHED

A PRATT DEMPCY & COMPANY
WESTERN ADVENTURE – BOOK 3

INSPIRED BY TRUE EVENTS

ORRIS SLADE

Cover Illustration by Tamara Schmidt

Contents

Prologue 6

Chapter 1 10

Chapter 2 18

Chapter 3 26

Chapter 4 34

Chapter 5 42

Chapter 6 50

Chapter 7 58

Chapter 8 65

Chapter 9 73

Chapter 10 82

Chapter 11 90

Chapter 12 98

Chapter 13 106

Chapter 14 114

Chapter 15 122

Chapter 16 130

Chapter 17 138

Epilogue 143

Prologue

Timber, California
September 1880

The saloon doors swung open. Budd Mansfield and Deputy Evan Farris stood in the entrance. Patrons turned to look in their direction. All but one.

Budd stepped into the saloon and pinned the man with a seething glare. He cleared his throat and pushed his hat up so that he could get a good look at his target. "Leroy Murphy," Budd drawled. "I've been chasing you down for three months."

"Well, I got a lot of enemies, so you better get in line," the outlaw grumbled into his glass before he took a swig. "What do you boys want, anyhow?"

The young deputy approached the table. "You are under arrest, Leroy Murphy, on suspicion of banditry." Evan took the glass from Leroy's hand and slammed a pair of cuffs onto the table.

Chairs scraped across the sticky saloon floor as the other patrons got to their feet. The music died on a strange note, and the working girls scurried out of sight. Six burly degenerates surrounded Evan and Budd, who had joined his deputy at Leroy's table.

Budd moved, so he and Evan were back-to-back. They surveyed the room and found no way out of their situation.

Either they gave up and walked out—unharmed and without their target—or they fought their way out with Leroy in hand. Budd reckoned he had a bit of fight left in him, even after several hours in the saddle. After all, their other leads had been dead ends, and he wasn't about to leave empty-handed again.

"Stand up, Murphy," Budd ordered. "And keep your hands where I can see them."

"I ain't goin' nowhere."

Budd placed his hand on Leroy's shoulder. The outlaw dug for his pistol and fired a shot just inches from Budd's face. Budd stumbled back, but recovered quickly. He kicked Leroy in the chest, sending the outlaw flying out of his chair. Leroy landed with a grunt and grabbed a whiskey bottle from the table beside him as he stood. Budd stepped to the side as the bottle hurled toward his head. It crashed behind the bar and shattered.

The unsavory-looking patrons charged at Evan and Budd.

"Every time we're on a job together, it ends in a shootout or a fist fight," Evan said with a big grin on his face. "Never a dull moment with you, Mansfield. "

"Keep your eyes on Leroy. He's a slippery weasel, and he'll tuck tail and run the second he sees an opportunity." Budd ducked and dodged one punch after another from various miscreants.

A tall, burly man grabbed Budd and slammed him on top of the bar. Budd smashed a glass over the man's head and rolled out of harm's way. Evan shouted for help a second later. Budd looked up and saw three nasty-looking outlaws surrounded his partner. He vaulted over the bar and launched himself at the first man in his path.

Leroy Murphy cowered behind someone's back, and Budd watched him inch his way closer to the back door. Budd whipped his pistol out of its holster. He fired a shot at Leroy, grazing the outlaw in the leg. Leroy crumbled to the floor with a pained yelp. Budd smiled for a moment before a devastating punch landed against his ribs, bringing him back to the fight. He jabbed his elbow into the man's side before he tossed him onto a table. The table broke beneath the man's weight. Shards of wood skittered across the floor.

"Farris, stop Leroy!" Budd shouted as they tackled him to the ground. He watched as Evan grabbed Leroy Murphy by the back of his jacket.

The outlaw put up a fight, but he was no match for the deputy. Budd tossed Evan the cuffs, and they landed near his feet. But another man who broke a stool over someone's back distracted Evan.

"Enough! "bellowed a voice from the doorway as they fired three shots into the air. Jordan Wicker, the new sheriff of Timber, eyed Evan with something akin to disappointment in his eyes. "I invited you into my town on good faith alone, and this is how you act, Deputy?"

Budd rammed his knee into an outlaw's belly, despite the sheriff's enraged demeanor. He walked over and pulled Leroy Murphy to his feet, ignoring the exchange between the lawmen. There was a job that needed doing: he clapped Leroy Murphy in irons and dragged him outside to where the horses waited. Budd's mare flicked her tail and gave him a sidelong glare as he hoisted the outlaw onto her back. He patted Ivory on her side and whispered a few sweet words to her before climbing into the saddle.

He secured the cuffs to the saddle horn. Leroy kicked up a fuss behind Budd. He shook the cuffs and hollered, "You may as well kill me! I ain't tellin' you nothin'!"

"You'll talk," Budd replied. "And when you give me the location of the gang's hideout, the safest place you could be is in a cell guarded by deputies."

"Wait a second… y-you… you're no lawman."

"I'm no bounty hunter either," Budd growled. "My name is Budd Mansfield, and I work for the Pratt and Dempcy stagecoach company."

There was silence as realization dawned upon Leroy, for his fate was in the hands of a man with no qualms about breaking the law in the name of justice. He worked in a delicate balance with lawmen, but he wore no badge. Budd's loyalty was to the victims of the Blood Eagle Gang, the innocent folks who were tormented by Leroy and his partners. "Now, I ain't gonna kill you," Budd muttered. "It might even force me to protect you if things turn sour, but I will make you talk."

Chapter 1

The Old Mill

Smoke had risen from beyond the tree line. Thick, black plumes roiled toward the sky as a flock of birds soared overhead. A lone rider sat astride his horse, looking down upon the small camp where his men awaited his arrival. Ripley Eagleson plucked a cigar from between his lips and exhaled slowly. He stubbed out the ember with the iron head of his saddle horn before tucking the cigar away. His allies had answered his call to arms.

He smiled behind the black scarf that covered the lower half of his face and urged his horse on. Storm tossed his mane and trotted along a narrow, winding path. The overgrown shrubs along the trail obscured most of the way ahead. Rip led the large stallion down to the valley at the base of the hill. They made their way over to the gate that surrounded the courtyard outside of the old steel mill.

Several years ago, a man who fancied himself a visionary had attempted to bring industry to the untamed west. It wasn't long before outlaws had run them out of the region. Years passed and construction never finished. The Old Mill was little more than a decrepit factory to most folks after a while. But to Rip and his gang, it was a fortress. Its walls protected them from attacks and provided shelter when they were forced to lie low. And with the insufferable Budd

Mansfield around, that was more often than not. There were stagecoaches in need of robbing, and yet the gang was forced to stay hunkered down until the law was off their trail.

"Boss," Charles called as Rip entered the courtyard. "Leroy is missin'. We haven't heard from him in weeks."

"Then we cut him loose," Rip replied as he lowered himself from the saddle. "I see we've gotten some responses from the others."

Charles nodded his head. "We sent ten letters and got four replies. Three of the four are already sendin' men to help us... but there's a problem."

"Isn't there always?" Rip snorted and hitched Storm to the post outside. He left his prized horse in the capable hands of their only servant and followed Charles inside. "What's the issue?"

"Valentine is in the city."

Rip stopped in his tracks. "Theodore Valentine is in Sacramento?"

"Yep. I saw him with my own two eyes." Charles lowered his voice to a whisper and moved closer to Rip. "I'm thinkin' Leroy goin' missin' ain't a coincidence. For all we know, Valentine might have him."

The last thing Rip needed was a rival gang in the area. Every time he crossed paths with Theodore Valentine and the Royal Heart Gang, it ended in bloodshed. Rip prided himself on the fact he was the sort of man who spared lives. But a war with Valentine would mean innocent folks getting caught in the crossfire. Ripley Eagleson was a cruel man but he was not a cold-blooded killer. He was on a personal mission to destroy Pratt & Dempcy. The profit he made in the stagecoach robberies along the way was just spoils of war. "Where's Valentine?" he asked.

"He's stayin' in a room at the hotel. There are guards outside the door, and God knows how many more of his men are in the city." Charles scowled down at his boots, looking rather deep in his thoughts. "Want me to send Sal?"

Salazar Torez was about as unhinged as a man could get. He enjoyed killing, savoring it like a fine wine. There was a darkness inside of Sal that the other men in Rip's gang just didn't possess. It made Sal the perfect tool to use against Valentine and Budd Mansfield. After all, Sal wasn't afraid to get his hands—or his knife—a little dirty.

"Send Sal into the city and have him watch over Valentine. See just how many men our old friend has here and report back to me," Rip ordered. "In the meantime, I have some business with Pete to attend to."

Hector Vasquez, Leroy Murphy, Salazar Torez, Charles Wright, and Pete Jones were Rip's most trusted men. He had known them for over a decade and fought by their side against their shared enemies. They were his brothers in arms, and yet if they knew the truth about where the loot was… Well, Rip just hoped that never happened. He had enough money to live a wealthy life somewhere with his sister and his young niece, but it was money that was supposed to have gone to the gang's families.

Rip was a no-good dirty swindler and a liar. He reckoned folks could have called him anything except a coward, and that was all right by him. Pete, however, was a coward. Several times, the young'un had Budd Mansfield in his sights and had failed to put the rabid dog down. That, in Rip's mind, was inexcusable. Pete should have gotten rid of Mansfield when he had the chance and saved them a lot of bullets.

An irritable groan left Rip as he pushed his way into the factory. Pete and Hector argued about something trivial near the back wall. Rip approached them calmly, listening to the rhythmic tapping of his polished shoes against the stone floor. He stopped a few feet away from Pete and Hector and smiled.

"Give us a moment, Hector," Rip said with a tight-lipped smile. "I need a word with our friend Pete. It'll only take a moment."

Hector tipped his hat and left them a second later. Rip waited until he heard the large iron door close before he called up his fist and slammed it against the wall near Pete's head. Pete flinched like the coward he was.

Rip grabbed Pete by the lapels of his jacket and yanked him close. "How long have you been working for Mansfield?" Rip sneered.

"I-I ain't!"

"No? Then why haven't you put a bullet in him yet?" Rip asked accusingly. "I saw you, Pete. Many times, you had Mansfield at your mercy, and you hesitated. Tell me why before I end you. Right. Now."

***

Sacramento, California

The morning seemed quiet when Budd first opened his eyes. He unfolded his long, achy limbs from the bed and shuffled over to the window. His calloused fingers pulled back the curtains. It was just before dawn, and the city hadn't quite woken yet. Only a few merchants milled about on their way into the shops, getting ready for a day's work.

Budd sighed and slipped his feet into a pair of old boots before he trudged downstairs. Evan was already awake with a steaming cup of coffee in his hand. Budd snatched the cup and downed the scalding, bitter liquid before his friend could protest. "Morning, Deputy," Budd chuckled as he took a seat at the table.

"A message came for you. Mr. Thayer wants to see you in his office immediately," Evan said. "I guess he finally found out what happened."

"Yeah, I suppose it was going to come to light eventually." Budd scrubbed a hand over his face and sighed. He loved his job when he wasn't chasing after the Blood Eagles. Last thing he wanted was to lose his place at Pratt & Dempcy. But mistakes were made, and Mr. Thayer most likely wanted answers.

"If he cuts you loose, I'm sure Sheriff Dawson would love to have you as a deputy," Evan replied, knowing very well Budd had no interest in being a lawman. "A badge might do you some good. Lord knows it's done wonders for me."

Budd snorted. "Is that what you keep telling yourself?" He grabbed a stale biscuit from the breadbasket on his way out the door and tossed a wave over his shoulder.

Sunlight peered over the hills, washing the city in hues of gray and amber. Budd took in the sight of the rising sun as he made his way down to Pratt & Dempcy. It was a small office attached to a private stable that housed wagons, carts, and stagecoaches.

Several of the men Budd hired to escort the coaches stood around near the stable doors. Work was slow because of the attacks on the road. The Blood Eagle Gang took the lives of innocent folks one too many times, and now some people just weren't willing to risk it. Not that Budd blamed them, but he knew it was no less dangerous than taking the train. Bandits were a plague upon this land, and it was left to men like Budd to clean up the mess. He tipped his hat to the men as he passed. The bell above the door chimed when he entered the office.

A young woman glanced up at Budd with a smile and pointed to a door to the left. "Mr. Thayer is waiting for you, Budd," she stated.

Budd mumbled his thanks and headed inside.

Mr. Thayer stood near the window of his office with his head low and his shoulders slumped in defeat. When he finally met Budd's gaze, there was a look of disappointment in his eyes. It hit Budd like a ton of bricks, for he hated to let anyone down—especially Mr. Thayer. Mr. Thayer sighed as he gestured to the seat across from his desk. "Why don't you sit down, son? We got some things to discuss."

"I already know what this is about," Budd admitted. "So, if you're going to fire me, I'd prefer if we do it standing."

Mr. Thayer slammed his palm into the desk. "I said sit down, Mansfield!" he shouted. It was unlike the kindhearted man to express any anger. "For once, just do what I ask."

Budd nodded. He raised his hands in surrender and took the offered seat. His weight caused the wood to groan, so he shifted around until he was comfortable. He stayed quiet as Mr. Thayer paced behind his desk. The sound of the clock ticking made Budd uneasy. He counted the seconds until Mr. Thayer spoke.

"You let them rob us," said Budd's employer. "You looked me in the eye for weeks and told me everything was under control, and that you were close to catching the bandits responsible for the attacks. And all this time… you allowed them to steal from our passengers. How long were you deceiving me? Was it the whole time?"

"No, of course not." Budd removed his hat and ran his fingers through his hair. He bounced his leg nervously, unsure of what was to come of all this. There were few things Budd considered worse than being fired from his job. Pratt & Dempcy took a chance on him when the world had chewed him up and spat him back out.

"Then when did it start?"

Budd took a deep breath and explained, "The gang leader reached out to me. Said he wanted to meet and put things to rest. I was ambushed and beaten."

"Go on."

"The gang leader gave me a choice," Budd continued. "Keep fighting and more people would die… or let the robberies happen and spare the lives onboard the stagecoaches."

Some of the anger left Mr. Thayer. It was clear in the way he breathed a sigh of relief. "I'm sorry," he said. "That can't have been an easy decision to make. For what it's worth... I would have made the same choice."

"It means a lot to hear you say that sir."

Mr. Thayer nodded slowly. "But next time something like that happens—"

"There won't be a next time," Budd reassured him. "Miss Dorothy Valentine and I agree the man responsible for the attacks is Ripley Eagleson."

"R-Ripley Eagleson?"

"He was here in town under the name of Reginald Pearce. You know him?" Budd asked.

"Ripley Eagleson used to work for Pratt and Dempcy."

Chapter 2

Glass shattered as a vase hit the wall. Water spilled along the floral pattern on the wallpaper. Shards of glass peppered the floor near the door of the bedchamber. A maid set down a platter of lamb and potatoes before she hurried out of the room.

The door closed with a bang that reverberated off the walls. Dotty Valentine stood before her fearsome father with a stubborn smile on her face. She had seen lawmen and criminals alike shrink beneath the might of Theodore Valentine's anger.

But Dotty had always held a special place in his heart. The only problem was that his love for her was rather smothering and overly protective. It was one reason Dotty had rebelled in her youth. But, alas, she had grown into a resourceful and dignified woman—she had him to thank for that.

"When your mother left us, I swore to protect you," he bellowed. "And I tried my best to do right by you, Dotty. I really have. And this is the thanks I get?"

Dotty shrugged her shoulders and took a seat on the edge of the bed. "I came to California, so you didn't have to deal with all this."

"Someone tried to slander my name!" Her father scribbled something on a slip of paper as he spoke. "I might be a wanted man, but I ain't never killed anybody who didn't deserve it. The Blood Eagles crossed a line when they drew our insignia."

"I know."

"And that Budd Mansfield," her father grumbled. "I don't care if he's a lawman or not, he had better stay out of my way or else."

Dotty's stomach twisted with dread, and her smile fell. "Please, Daddy. Don't harm him. He only wishes to help."

Theodore must have sensed something in her voice. He stood up from the writing desk in the corner of the hotel room and placed a hand on Dotty's arm. He said, "Let it go, darling. Whatever *feelings* may have been stirred up by Mansfield... let them go. Loving a man tied up with outlaws is a life of misery. It's why I never blamed your mother for leaving when she did."

Dotty felt the heat of the flush on her cheeks. "I-I... you must be mistaken. There's nothing between me and Mr. Mansfield. We are working together to put an end to the Blood Eagle Gang. That's all, Daddy."

Her father shook his head and replied, "I know more than you think I do. I know he took you in when the people in this city turned their noses up at you."

"He did, yes."

"I also know Mansfield took a chance on you despite you being my daughter," he said. "But he's a dangerous man, and he ain't good enough for you even on his best day."

"It ain't like that." Dotty brushed a hand over her skirt nervously. She felt the weight of her father's gaze. It was like he had seen right through her. "Besides, we've done good work together. One of our leads even helped him capture that awful Leroy Murphy."

"Murphy is not my priority. Ripley Eagleson is. And I fully intend to bury him six feet under before I leave Sacramento," her father replied. "Budd Mansfield would be smart to stay out of it. Rip and I… we go way back. We've always known this feud would end in a bad way. Whether the Royal Hearts or the Blood Eagles walk away from this fight, I want you as far from the gunfire as possible."

Dotty shook her head and grabbed her father's hand. "I'll be right there in the middle of the excitement, and you know that. I'm a Valentine, Daddy. We don't run from anything or anybody." She glanced back at the chair near the writing desk. "Now, why don't you tell me about Ripley Eagleson?"

Her father pulled the chair closer and sat down. He took her hand in his and said, "We worked together, Rip and I. Not the way you would think, either. He was a driver for Pratt and Dempcy and I was just another bandit on the road."

Dotty's jaw dropped.

"For years we set up ambushes together. I'd rob the stagecoaches, and he'd steal the insurance money from the safe in Thayer's office. It was a smooth operation."

His words conjured a hoard of conflicting emotions inside of Dotty. "What changed? How did you become enemies?"

"Rip got greedy," he scoffed. "He started taking more than we agreed on. Started hiding it from me. One day, he took too much, and Mr. Thayer found out money had gone missing from the safe. It didn't take long after that for him to realize Rip was the culprit. After he was arrested, Rip gave me up to the sheriff in return for his freedom. Lawmen figured a bandit was worth more than a petty thief."

"And Ripley Eagleson is back to robbing stagecoaches. For what reason, though? Revenge?" Dotty wondered aloud. "It all seems so..."

"Simple?" Her father chuckled. "You were expecting more than an impish tantrum from a man like Rip? He's a cunning thief, and that's it. His real power comes from the gang. He plays them like puppets on a string."

Dotty chewed on her bottom lip in concentration. "Where is all the money?"

"What?"

"He's hiding out in the Old Mill with a gang of outlaws. Where is he keeping the money stolen during the stagecoach robberies?" Dotty asked her father. A frown etched itself upon her lovely features as she pondered to herself.

Theodore snapped his fingers and said, "Beatrice. His sister was always the person he trusted the most. If anyone is hiding the money, it's her."

"If I can find Beatrice, perhaps I can convince her to return the stolen goods," Dotty suggested. She struggled to imagine any respectable woman would approve of such behavior.

***

Outskirts of Sacramento, California

Budd slowed his horse to a stop outside of a hovel. The walls bowed outward as they struggled to hold up the weight of the roof. An outcrop of stone concealed the shack's location.

The large rocks cast an enormous shadow over the lopsided little structure. It was hard for Budd to believe someone had tried to build a home out here.

He pushed open the brittle door and saw Leroy Murphy shackled on the floor. Evan stood over the outlaw with a furious look on his face.

"What happened?" Budd asked. "What did he say?"

"He's been talking about all the killings. Says *things just happened on the road* and we should let him go." Evan wiped the sweat from his brow and said, "Innocent folks have died because of him and the rest of his gang."

Budd nodded his head and crouched down beside Leroy. He tilted the outlaw's head back and looked into his dark gaze. "They killed good men trying to protect those coaches," Budd growled. "Some of them have families still waiting for justice to be served. Now, I like to think I'm an excellent judge of character... and you don't strike me as the sort of man who would lay down his life for someone else."

Leroy Murphy spat near Budd's boots. "That's what I think of your justice."

Budd balled up his fist and slammed it into Leroy's jaw so hard that the outlaw's head whipped to the side. He shook his hand to rid himself of the ache in his knuckles. "Who else is in the gang?" Budd questioned. "Ripley Eagleson, Salazar Torez, Charles Wright... stop me if I make a mistake."

"I work alone."

There was a moment when Budd's vision turned red with anger. But he wasn't the heartless man he used to be. He reined in his control and reached into his pocket and pulled out a stack of cards.

They were the Ace of Spades cards he collected from each of the robbed stagecoaches. They had pinned each card in place with a throwing knife, like some sort of signature for the gang. Several were spattered with blood.

Budd flicked the cards at Leroy, one at a time. "I'm only going to ask you one more time. If you don't give me the answers I need, I'll ask my friend here to take off his badge and look the other way," he stated firmly. "I'm not a patient man, Leroy. I've been known to lose my temper when questioning outlaws."

Leroy gulped nervously.

"I used to work for the Pinkertons," Budd revealed. "Folks used to call me their hunting dog. But when they set me loose on a jumpy, spineless criminal like you... they called me a monster. Do you understand what I'm getting at?"

Leroy remained quiet, but he nodded his head. His eyes darted around the hovel as if he were searching for a way out. But there was no escaping Budd Mansfield.

"Who else is in the gang?" Budd sneered. "Give me names." A second punch knocked Leroy onto his side. It was followed by a third and fourth punch, ending with a sickening crunch as the outlaw's nose broke.

"All right! I'll tell you!"

Budd stopped. His arm was cocked back, ready to hit Leroy again if he stayed quiet. "Names, Leroy. Give me names, or this continues."

"If I tell you... they'll kill me. Traitors don't last long around these parts." Leroy lifted his shackled hands and forced his nose back into place. A blood-curdling shriek filled the air. He panted heavily. "I'll tell you... if you give your word that, I'll go free."

Budd hesitated. He glanced over his shoulder at his partner, and Evan gave a curt nod. "You got a deal."

"Pete Jones. Pete, Hector Vasquez," he panted, "Charles Wright, Salazar Torez... And Ripley Eagleson."

Once the names left Leroy's lips, Budd yanked him to his feet. He dragged Leroy out to the horses and tossed him over the back of Ivory.

Budd knocked Leroy unconscious to keep the outlaw from throwing himself off. "Head to town ahead of me, so no one suspects anything," he told Evan. "I'll be home before sunset."

"Are you really going to let him go free?" Evan asked.

"No. I'm handing him over to Sheriff Dawson the second I get to town." Budd dug a cigarette out of his pocket, lit the end with a match, and took a long drag. "Either he hangs, or he rots in a jailhouse cell. Either way, there'll be a blizzard in the desert before I let another criminal go free." He clicked his tongue and urged Ivory back toward the road.

A puff of smoke curled out of his nostrils as they rode back to Sacramento. Budd took his time, rolling the names of the bandits around in his head.

He hoped the long ride would summon a memory to the front of his mind. Something that might explain why the name Salazar Torez caused a stirring of hatred in his gut.

Dotty had told him Salazar and Charles once worked for her father, but she failed to mention who they were before they turned up in California. Budd knew there was more digging to be done.

He turned onto the main road that cut through town and entered Sacramento. Those who knew him waved, and those who feared him kept moving with their heads down. It still shocked him just how many folks were supportive of the bandits who robbed the stagecoaches.

Ripley Eagleson had garnered quite the sparkling reputation under the name of Reginald Pearce.

Some people were unwilling to believe their community hero was a dirty, rotten outlaw. Even so, Budd kept riding until he came upon the sheriff's office. Dawson was waiting outside when he arrived.

The lawman greeted Budd with a tip of his hat and a tight-lipped smile as he approached the horse. "I guess I could waste both of our time and ask what happened to his face," Sheriff Dawson said. "But I suppose some things are better left as they are. No need to go asking questions I don't want the answer to."

"That's a good thing to live by Sheriff."

Chapter 3

En route to Black Lake, California

The wagon rolled into view. Rip tugged his mask into place, and his men followed suit. They waited on their horses, watching closely until the wagon approached the ambush site.

Rip gave the signal, and the five riders in black charged. Storm pulled up beside the wagon as the driver gave a shout.

"Stop now!" Rip ordered. He disguised his voice with a deep, exaggerated drawl. The driver snapped the reins and pulled ahead of the dark stallion.

Rip spurred Storm on and caught up in the blink of an eye. He flipped his revolver out of the holster and ordered the driver to stop once more.

The wagon slowed.

Pete and Hector leaped into the back of the wagon. Their horses followed closely, unwilling to leave their riders. Salazar threw a knife at the shotgun man.

The man shouted and dropped the gun as the knife embedded itself into his hand. Charles whistled once just as the wagon stopped, signaling there was a second wagon nearby.

Rip climbed down from his saddle and walked over to the passengers Hector had lined up. A man dropped to his knees and babbled on and on in German. Rip couldn't understand a word the man said, so he tapped his gun in warning.

The German scrambled around. He reached down for a coin purse with only seven dollars inside. It was pitiful, really.

"What's in the back?" Rip asked his men.

Hector scoffed and dumped out the contents of a bag. Only a few articles of clothing and a handful of photographs dropped onto the ground. "There's nothing here, boss."

"Nothin' in the strongbox, neither," said Pete.

Rip pushed the man's hand away and dug around in his satchel for a stack of cash. He tossed it to the German man. Immediately, the man cried as he thanked Rip profusely.

Words of gratitude spilled from his lips. The man's family even cried and praised him. Their adoration filled Rip with a profound sense of righteousness.

"Pack up your things and get yourselves to town," Rip said. "We ain't robbin' from the poor." He waited until the family filled the wagon and rode away before he released the driver and the shotgun man. Rip forced the Pratt & Dempcy workers to walk back to Sacramento with nothing more than a half-empty canteen of water.

"We let them go?" Salazar hissed. "What if they send someone after us?"

"Easy," Rip replied. "Check your tone before I lose my temper."

Salazar stood toe to toe with Rip. He cursed under his breath in Spanish before backing down. But there was an edge to his voice as he said, "There's a second wagon. Let's get ready for it, compadres."

The men stared between Rip and Sal. There was an uncomfortable silence that fell over the gang as they hopped back into their saddles.

Rip led the men to where Charles had been surveying the land. He looked over the hill at the flat expanse of desert and saw a lone wagon stopped near a patch of dead, brittle shrubs. Rip gave Sal and Hector the signal to approach from the east.

Charles and Pete followed Rip as he took the direct path to the wagon. He removed his scarf and tucked it into the breast pocket of his coat.

"Afternoon, miss," he said to the young woman as he neared the wagon. "You seem to be havin' some trouble with that." Rip nodded toward the three gentlemen, who were trying their hardest to put the wheel back onto the wagon.

"Golly! I wasn't expecting to see anyone out in this miserable heat." She flicked open a fan and attempted to cool herself. "The wheel just came off as we came around the bend. My husband and the driver—" Her voice cut off with a squeak as Sal pressed a knife to her cheek.

"Scream and I'll carve you up," Sal threatened. "Where's the money?"

Her eyes darted to the wagon. It was all Hector, and the others needed. They held the three men at gunpoint while Pete searched the wagon.

Usually, Leroy would have broken open the strongbox. Without him, the gang was forced to take the box with them hoping to crack it open later. Rip barked out orders as the men ransacked the wagon.

Sal threatened the woman's husband until he gave up a gold-plated pocket watch. Rip snagged the watch for himself, silently daring anyone to question him.

Though Sal looked as if he wanted to argue, the gang stayed quiet. It was best not to get on Ripley Eagleson's bad side.

"We got gold!" shouted Hector. He hefted a trunk onto the ground and opened the lid. Hidden among a bunch of suits were three little golden nuggets. The men must have been prospectors headed into town to see an assayer.

"Check for trinkets," Rip told his men. He watched them rummage through the many bags until Pete found a handful of fine jewelry and a stack of love letters.

"She's Sheriff Dawson's bride," Pete informed the others. "He'll be expectin' her to arrive any minute now. We gotta get out of here!"

Rip took the woman by the arm. "Forget my face," he said darkly.

The woman nodded quickly and yanked her arm out of his grasp. "You got what you came for," she hissed. "Just go."

There was a part of Rip that wanted to punish the woman for her show of defiance. Instead, Rip took the stack of letters from Pete. "Speak a word of this to the sheriff, and I'll come find you," he said as he tucked the letters into his satchel.

***

A knock at the door came in the early hours of the morning. Budd climbed out of bed with a groan and opened the door. Dotty pushed her way into his bedchamber.

Budd straightened his shirt and glared at the brazen young woman. "Most ladies would be opposed to barging into a man's sleeping quarters, Miss Valentine," he muttered. "I don't recall requesting your presence this morning."

"Oh, enough already," she said with a dismissive wave of her hand. "We have a problem, Mr. Mansfield."

Budd felt the corner of his mouth lift into an amused smirk. "I'd say," he replied. "The daughter of Theodore Valentine is standing in my room, and a war between two rival gangs has torn this city apart. What more could go wrong?"

"The man who saved you… Reginald Pearce is—"

"Ripley Eagleson?" Budd interjected. "I already know. Your father made the same claim. I'm not sure what to believe. Reginald might not be who you think he is."

Dotty's fiery stare locked onto Budd's gaze. "My father wouldn't have said anything about it if it wasn't the truth. He's not a liar."

"He's a criminal, Dotty." Budd crossed his arms over his chest and leaned against the wall. "Not exactly the sort of person I extend my trust to."

"So am I. A criminal, I mean. And so were Evan Ferris and Blake Wright and his brothers."

Budd held his breath as she stepped closer to him. "That's different," he argued. "You were born into this life. And the others were just caught up in dangerous situations."

She shook her head. "I don't blame my father for who I've become. I chose this path just as you have."

Budd hadn't realized just how close Dotty had gotten until her nose brushed his. He leaped out of her reach and moved away from the wall, keeping her at arm's length.

The smell of roses was strong in the air, filling his senses until he knew nothing but her scent. Budd shook his head to clear his mind and swallowed thickly. Brazen women made him nervous, but Dotty was downright reckless.

"Mr. Mansfield, the only way to know for certain is to ask Mr. Pearce himself," she said pointedly. "Shall we take a stroll across town?"

Budd followed Dotty down to the front door. He put on his boots and coat before he stepped outside into the first light of dawn.

Evan, Sheriff Dawson, and Dotty had the bad habit of waking him before the rooster crowed. Budd reckoned he'd sleep when he was dead, so there was no use in being upset. He prided himself on having an even temperament most days.

But there were times, like when Leroy Murphy had been questioned, that Budd lost his temper. Nothing good ever came from him losing control.

Still, he walked arm in arm with Dotty Valentine until they reached the heart of the city. Budd then put a respectable distance between them.

Though she cared little about her reputation, Budd wasn't willing to scandalize a woman who deserved the respect of her peers—not that a woman as incredible and fearless as Dotty Valentine had equals. She was truly one of a kind. Budd just hoped she wasn't dragged down with her father.

"There's Sheriff Dawson," Dotty announced. A furrow creased her brow. "He doesn't look too happy this morning."

The sheriff waved them down. Dawson scratched at his stubbled chin and shivered as if he had been reliving something awful. "I'm glad I spotted you two," he grumbled. "There was a body out by Pine's Bluff."

"A body?" Budd questioned. "The only person missing is... the telegram operator. Bill Weston's son."

"He was found with this." Sheriff Dawson held up a yellowed telegram with his own name signed at the bottom. "This message was intended for the marshal's office. I never heard back from them. Now I know why."

"Got any leads?" Dotty asked.

Dawson's expression grew dark. He stood up straighter and looked Budd in the eyes as he said, "There was only one person I told about the telegram. And that was John Pepper's brother-in-law Reginald Pearce."

Budd removed his hat and raked his fingers through his hair roughly. He thought back to the day Reginald had saved his life. Had it all been a setup? Could Ripley Eagleson have been right in front of him all along?

He wondered about these things to himself. Budd felt his doubt lessen. Though he had wanted Theodore Valentine to be mistaken, there was no denying the facts.

"Try to contact the marshal's office again," Budd told the sheriff. "See if they can send someone. I'll head to the jailhouse and question Leroy."

Sheriff Dawson opened his mouth to argue but stopped himself. He gave Budd a nod and pressed his lips into a thin line. The lawman practically vibrated with tension. Budd wasn't surprised.

The mayor had Dawson under a lot of pressure to get this gang in shackles. The Blood Eagle Gang was smarter than any group of bandits Budd had ever faced. Catching them seemed almost impossible.

Dotty gave the sheriff a small, sympathetic smile before pulling Budd aside. "Have you gone mad?" she whispered. "A marshal will recognize my father."

"We can't keep them in the dark forever," Budd replied. "Something big is brewing in these parts, and we need all the help we can get. Make sure your father is careful. I'll deal with the law."

Dotty placed her hand on his arm. "Thank you, Mr. Mansfield. You've been a decent friend to me and keeping my father out of trouble is the least I can do to repay you."

"That's what partners do, ain't it?" He removed her hand from his arm and left her with Sheriff Dawson. Budd trekked to the edge of town, where the jailhouse sat in isolation.

Chapter 4

The door opened, and Budd was hit with the stench of sweat and mold. He stepped into the darkened interior, eyes scanning the shadows for signs of life.

Sunlight spilled in through the bars on the small window near the ceiling. The light illuminated the bearded face of Leroy Murphy.

Leroy sat up when he noticed Budd in the doorway. "Come to watch me rot away in this cell?"

"I'm not interested in what happens to you, Leroy." Budd shook his head and approached the cell. He curled his lip in disgust at the filth he saw inside. Sheriff Dawson's deputies had provided Leroy with a bucket, water, and food for the day. However, it was clear Leroy lacked a general understanding of cleanliness. "I'm here to talk about your boss."

"And why should I tell you anythin' after you locked me away in here?"

"Because Ripley Eagleson's days in Sacramento Valley are numbered," Budd explained. "Either you can help us, and I can put in a good word with the marshal, or you can stay quiet until Rip sends somebody to make sure you don't make it to trial."

"What do you want to know?" Leroy sat up with his back against the wall and his legs stretched out in front of him.

"Where does the money go?"

"We got families," Leroy said. "Rip sends the loot out of California with his sister, and she makes sure it gets to our families."

Budd doubted a man as greedy and vindictive as Ripley Eagleson had a crime operation built on good intentions. In fact, Budd was willing to wager the gang's families never saw a penny of the money stolen from the stagecoaches. "The attack on Calligan Road. Tell me about that."

Leroy smiled as he scratched at his scraggly beard. "That one was the boss's idea. He's brilliant, you know? Smarter than anyone around here. You think you can catch him? He'll just make a fool out of you... again."

"The attack, Leroy."

"Some of us were passengers. Some were guards," the outlaw chuckled. "We hid right under your nose. You didn't suspect a thing."

Budd cursed under his breath. Blake had been right. The whole thing had been staged—an attempt to throw the law off the Blood Eagle Gang's trail. And it worked.

Well, at least until a witness had identified Leroy Murphy. The Murphy family had been a pain in Sheriff Dawson's rear for a long time. Their family was known for being thieves and swindlers.

"What can you tell me about the Old Mill?" Budd questioned. "How does the gang keep it secure?"

"Ain't like the location is a secret, Mansfield," Leroy snorted. "It's the terrain that keeps us safe. The walls are surrounded by rough, untamed forest and steep hills. Folks don't dare venture that far into the forest. Those old paths were covered in a rockslide not long after construction on the factory stopped."

"I need a way in."

Leroy stood up and shuffled over to the bars. He leaned forward and said, "I *could* tell ya. But I'll need a few beers to keep me warm at night."

"I ain't cuttin' deals."

"Then I ain't talkin'." Leroy turned to leave.

Budd grabbed the back of the outlaw's sweat-soaked shirt and slammed him against the bars. He wrapped his arm around Leroy's neck through the bars. Leroy kicked his legs and gasped for breath.

Budd pressed his forearm against Leroy's throat and whispered, "You want me to snap? Is that it? You want to see what happens when I lose control?"

Leroy gurgled and shook his head, hands clawing at Budd's arm.

"You ready to talk now?"

There was a subtle nod.

Budd released Leroy and stepped away from the cell. "How do I find the trail?"

Leroy coughed as he hit the floor. He gripped his neck and wheezed heavily, trying to catch his breath. "The path is hard to find. You won't see it the first time you're out there. Head southeast once you reach Yosemite Valley. It's a two-day ride from the river."

Budd heard the door open.

Blake and Steven Wright entered the jailhouse. Smiles spread across their faces as they took in the sight of Leroy sputtering on the floor. Steven grabbed a small stool and took guard outside of Leroy's cell. Blake requested to speak with Budd in private.

They walked out the back door of the jailhouse to a water trough, where the deputies hitched their horses.

"I can't just sit around waitin' for another attack," Blake said. "I want to be out there with you and Evan, huntin' these criminals down."

"How well do you know the area around Yosemite Valley?"

"As well as anyone, I guess," Blake replied. "Steep rock formations, abandoned mines, dense forest, rapids, waterfalls, and there's a few cave systems too."

"Do you know anything about an old mining trail that—"

"You want me to go to the Old Mill?" The former outlaw's eyes went wide.

"I take it you've been there."

Blake shook his head. "Not personally, but my brother Charles talked about it. Said it was near impossible to find."

Budd glanced around to make sure they were alone. He dropped his voice low and said, "Well, I need you to find it. And I need you to look at what we might deal with as far as defenses and ambush points."

"You thinkin' of an attack?" Blake asked.

"We might not have a choice. Once the marshal gets here, Sheriff Dawson will want to do things by the book. That means formal arrests." Budd reached into his satchel and pulled out a scrap of paper and a pencil.

He scribbled down the directions Leroy Murphy gave him before he handed it over to Blake. "If you don't send word in three days, I'm comin' to find you. I ain't losin' another good man to this gang."

"You got it, boss."

Budd clapped Blake on the shoulder. "In the meantime, I got bandits to hunt."

***

Black Lake, California

A man crashed through the inn window and landed on the sidewalk. Glass covered the ground, crunching as Budd Mansfield climbed through the broken frame and yanked the man to his feet.

He dragged the outlaw over to a barrel of water beside the front door and dunked his head inside. A crowd formed as the drowning man kicked up a fuss. Budd let up after a few seconds.

He allowed the man to take a shallow breath before he dunked him back under.

Dirty fingernails dug into Budd's hand as he lifted his prey out of the water once more. "You owe me an explanation, Pete Jones," Budd snarled. His shirt was drenched, and so were his boots.

"Sheriff Dawson let you go because we had nothing on you, but you gave him your word you wouldn't show your face in this territory again!"

"I ain't have a choice. My boss... h-he suspected I had turned yellow!" Pete's bloodshot eyes were full of panic. "He would have killed me dead if I tried to leave."

Budd reached for Pete again, but someone grabbed his arm. He had been so caught up in the interrogation that he hadn't noticed when Evan rode up.

His partner flashed his deputy badge and told the crowd to leave. Budd led Pete around back where prying eyes were less likely to see them talking. Evan followed closely on Budd's heels, ready to intervene if necessary.

Pete's back hit the exterior wall of the inn in the blink of an eye. "All right, all right," he sniveled. "I'll tell you anythin'. Just don't hurt me."

"Why are you in Black Lake?" Evan asked.

"I came to give Mansfield a message," answered Pete. The outlaw then turned his gaze to Budd. "The boss has gone mad. He's goin' on about retribution and settin' things right. None of us know when he'll lose it, but it won't be long. He's crazy."

An unstable Ripley Eagleson meant Budd was in for a terrible week. "What's he got planned?" Budd inquired irritably. "Another stagecoach attack?"

Pete shook his head. "He wants to attack Black Lake. Says it's a big payday if we can pull it off. I ain't too sure I want to attack a town, Mr. Mansfield. That's too big for me. My family lives in these parts. Folks know me around here. It's too much."

Budd took a deep breath and steadied himself. He dropped his hand onto Pete's shoulder, resisting the urge to squeeze more information out of the outlaw. "What exactly did Rip say?"

There was a moment when he thought Pete would have withheld the information. The young man had a reputation for being cowardly. But to Budd's surprise, Pete stood his ground and handed Budd a letter written by Ripley Eagleson himself.

It was instructions for Pete to survey the town, to keep notes on the lawmen and the comings and goings of prominent members of the community. Though there was no mention of an attack in the letter, it was quite clear to Budd what Ripley's intentions were.

"Attacking a town will take more than five outlaws," Budd muttered. Pete's silence struck him as odd, so Budd pressed further. "Unless... Ripley Eagleson has gotten himself a bigger gang since the last time we crossed paths. Pete?"

"The boss cashed in a few favors. Louis Bennett, Gerald Isaac, and Berry Newman sent men to help. I reckon there's nearly twenty camped out at the Old Mill. More show up every day"

Budd's heart stopped for a second. He felt as if the world had suddenly grown darker and far too small for his comfort. Ripley Eagleson had terrorized the region with only five riders.

Budd knew just how much damage the man could do with thirty. The prospect shook Budd. He was almost tempted to telegraph the Pinkertons for help. But not even an army of outlaws could have made Budd that desperate.

"Get back to your post and say nothing about this conversation," Budd said to Pete. "If folks ask, tell them I caught you cheating at the card tables and came to collect. I mean it, Pete. Keep your head down and your nose out of trouble."

"Y-yes, sir." The young man scampered off, leaving Budd and Evan alone in the alley behind the inn.

Evan gave Budd a look of concern. "Twenty outlaws… we're outnumbered, Budd. Black Lake, Timber, and Sacramento combined only have about ten deputies. Even if we pull together on this, it'll be an all-out war."

"Valentine has men."

"Do you really want to involve Dotty's father?" Evan asked. "We need a plan, and fast. Last thing we need is to get dry-gulched by Ripley Eagleson and his gang."

"Black Lake is a small town. We can shelter folks in the church if we have to," Budd replied. "I'll talk to Valentine and ask what he knows about the attack. You see if Dawson will lend some men to guard Black Lake."

Evan nodded. "Be safe, friend."

"You too, partner." Budd crossed the road and wandered toward the saloon. He crept inside and made his way to the back rooms, where patrons played cards. Budd knocked on the third door and heard Valentine's deep, raspy voice beckon him inside. He pushed his way into the room and stepped through a cloud of cigar smoke.

"I wasn't aware I invited you to this private game," Valentine said. "To what do I owe this pleasure?"

"We need to talk about Dotty," Budd answered. He pulled out a chair from the card table and took a seat. "She's persistent and headstrong. And if Ripley Eagleson sees an opportunity to gain leverage over you—"

"Over *us*, Mr. Mansfield," Valentine interjected. "Don't insult my intelligence by suggesting you harbor no feelings for my daughter."

Chapter 5

Three days had come and gone without so much as a single arrest. Dotty paced anxiously around her hotel room. The only thing that kept her busy was spying on her father.

His days were filled with secret meetings, obsessive gun collecting, and card games. It was all quite boring, really. Dotty had been the face of the Royal Hearts for nearly five years, but she assumed her father had maintained some of his influence.

Instead, it seemed he was quite happy to let her run things despite their countless arguments on the contrary.

It had taken a long time for her to gain the gang's respect. Hard work and determination had gotten her far. Perhaps Ripley Eagleson had done the same at one point.

After all, Dotty heard a few ladies gossiping in town about bandits who attacked a wagon, only to *give* the passenger money. It was an odd story, but not something unusual for Ripley Eagleson.

To Dotty's knowledge, Ripley Eagleson only had his eye on revenge against Pratt & Dempcy. Something she figured might change if her father got involved.

Dotty sighed and plopped herself down in a chair. She wanted to be with Budd, hunting outlaws and fighting off bandits. But he had given her the job of watching her father, which meant she was stuck sitting idly by as the excitement was outside.

The hotel was too quiet. She glanced over at the clock on the wall and groaned when she saw the time. It was well after midnight when Dotty noticed her father's return from Black Lake.

She heard his voice out near the stables behind the hotel. Dotty moved closer to the window after she doused the lamp. She hid in the shadows, watching through the curtains as her father stood in a circle with a strange group of men. The strike of a match illuminated her father's face with an amber glow.

"Ripley Eagleson ain't gonna let Leroy go to trial," said Theodore. "He'll attack the stagecoach before it ever makes it to Reno."

"Hector Vasquez was seen in Timber. Drank a little too much and started goin' on and on about the ambush," added the man to Theodore's left.

Dotty's lips parted on a gasp. She grabbed her robe from the chair and pulled it on, fastening it tight. Her fingers trembled as she adjusted her bonnet. Slippers tapped upon the wooden floors.

Dotty shuffled across the room and headed outside through the back door. The stairs creaked quietly. Her father's voice grew quiet as he walked around the corner with his associates. Dotty followed, clinging to the wall of the hotel.

"If Eagleson is anythin' like I remember, he'll slaughter the guards and ride off with the coach before anybody knows what's what," a strange man said as he twirled a thin mustache.

Dotty's gaze flickered between the man and her father. Theodore scratched his trimmed beard and replied, "We'll stay out of it. Let the sheriff deal with the prisoner. We need to prepare to take on Eagleson if he decides he wants to go through with this war."

War? Dotty shook her head in disbelief. Her father was up to no good, as usual, and that spelled bad news for Budd Mansfield. She snuck past the alleyway and ducked behind the general store.

Luckily, her father hadn't caught sight of her hasty retreat. Dotty followed the contours of the buildings until there was nothing but an open road between her and Budd's home.

She walked swiftly toward the little house at the edge of town. Ivory flicked her tail and snickered as Dotty passed the barely tamed mare.

The door opened before Dotty knocked. Budd stood in the doorway with a knowing grin on his face. "A bit late for visitors, Miss Valentine," he chuckled quietly. "What can I do for you?"

Dotty licked her lips nervously and said, "You're transporting Leroy Murphy at dawn, aren't you?"

Guilt flashed in Budd's gaze and his smile faded. "I am."

"You weren't going to tell me," she said. "Like my father, you assume I'm better off not knowing."

"It ain't like that."

"We're partners, Budd," Dotty snapped. "You said so yourself. I'm going with you. Argue against it if you like, but

I've been given permission from Sheriff Dawson to accompany you and your men on travels."

"I don't work for the sheriff."

"If I'm not there to spot an ambush, you won't be working for the stagecoach company, either." Dotty's retort seemed to break through Budd Mansfield's stubbornness. "A man told my father the gang is planning an ambush. My father has no intention of telling the sheriff or intervening."

"Does he know when it'll happen?" Budd asked.

Dotty shook her head. "The man only said it'll happen long before the coach makes it to Reno."

"And there are plenty of ambush points." Budd stepped out onto the porch and shut the door behind him. He leaned his back against a wooden beam and crossed his arms over his chest. "We were going to take a road through Yosemite that Blake Wright found."

Dotty moved closer to Budd. She felt waves of heat permeating from his large body as she stood in front of him. "I can hide in the back of the coach if that will put your mind at ease..."

"You'll ride up front with me," Budd stated firmly. He dropped his arms to his side and squeezed his hands into tight fists. "I don't want you anywhere near Leroy Murphy. No, you stay with me."

"Then what is the plan?"

Budd shifted closer and craned his neck downward, so he was only inches from her ear. "The only thing I'm thinking about now is keeping you by my side," he said. His voice was little more than a deep rumble. "Do you trust me, Dotty? Do you trust I'll keep you safe?"

"I trust you, Budd," she said. "But I can keep myself safe."

***

En Route to Reno, Nevada

Budd snapped the reins, and the stagecoach jolted forward. He whispered calmly to the horses as he steered them toward the forest. The scent of pine filled his nostrils. Trees sprawled over steep, rolling hills.

Budd heard a waterfall in the distance. He thought back to the day when the river in Yosemite Valley had dragged him over the rushing rapids and down a frightening drop of a waterfall. Budd hadn't been able to go near a river since without reliving the horror of nearly drowning.

A touch on his arm snapped him back to reality. Budd looked to his right and saw Dotty cleaning her pistols. There was a look of concern in her eyes that baffled him. Perhaps he wasn't as good at hiding his emotions as he thought. "Why are you here?" Budd asked her. "Why have you risked your father's anger to help me?"

"Because I believe I am falling in love with you, Budd Mansfield."

Budd was taken aback by her honesty. His face turned red, and the tips of his ears felt as if they were on fire.

But the respect he felt for her overwhelmed his embarrassment. "Thank you for that, Miss—er—Dotty."

Dotty's hand returned to his arm as she gazed up at him with adoration glittering in her hazel eyes. Budd felt the radiance of her smile reach down into his soul. It thawed a bit of the bitterness that had rested inside of him for so long.

Perhaps all that had transpired wasn't so bad. Perhaps there was some good he could look forward to on the other side.

Blake Wright rode up to Budd and pointed to the spot where the road broke off to a system of paths. "I trekked each one by foot. Ain't no way the outlaws took any of them. If the Old Mill really is still out here... I ain't found it yet."

Budd jerked his head toward a smokestack in the distance. "Maidu?"

Blake nodded. "The tribe wasn't too happy to see me trudgin' across their land."

"It's a risk, but we can contact them. We could make an offering and see if they can tell us where to find Ripley Eagleson's hideaway," Budd wondered aloud.

He wasn't in search of any particular answer. "Did you see any ambush spots ahead?"

"There's a few I'm concerned about," said Blake. "Once we clear the forest, we'll be out in the open. Which means we won't have cover if we take on gunfire."

"If the Blood Eagle Gang is planning an attack on the stagecoach *and* the town, that must mean they have more men than Pete thought," Dotty added. "Something doesn't feel right about this."

"We can handle it." Budd steered the coach along the road that veered off to the left. He kept his eyes on the tree line, watching for any sign of movement. He heard Dotty reloading her pistols before she returned them to their holsters.

Every shadow, every rustle of the underbrush, every voice that carried through the forest drew his attention. But it wasn't until they broke through the edge of the forest that Budd saw something out of the ordinary.

A rider, alone and draped in black, sat upon a gray shire horse at the center of the path. Budd gripped the reins until his knuckles cracked. "You got a bead on him, Dotty?" He asked.

"He's in my sights."

"Then hold on tight," Budd said as he snapped the reins hard. The horses bolted toward the rider. Dotty kept her arm straight even as the stagecoach wobbled. Budd stared down the road at the rider. He whistled sharply, signaling the others.

Blake, Steven, and Evan charged after the coach. Bullets flew from the trees, popping holes in the walls of the stagecoach. Leroy Murphy shouted above the gunfire.

The outlaw threw his weight to one side as the coach turned and knocked it off balance. A wheel came off and rolled to the side.

Budd held on as the stagecoach tipped over. "Cover us!" he shouted as they hit the ground.

Dotty rolled away from the upturned coach and fired at the rider. Blake jumped from his horse and dragged Leroy Murphy behind a tree.

The outlaw tripped over his shackles. Steven moved to his brother's side as Evan helped Budd from the wreckage. Three more riders appeared on the road.

"We're in trouble," Dotty called out. She shot at the riders, causing them to scatter for cover. There was a cut above her brow, but she was otherwise unhurt.

The bullets spooked the first rider's horse, and it bucked him out of the saddle. Dotty rushed him immediately, kicking his gun out of reach.

Budd climbed to his feet. His heart stopped when he saw sunlight glint off the sharp edge of a knife as the rider tackled Dotty. He flipped his revolver out of the holster and shot the knife out of the rider's hand.

The man yelped and jumped back. Dotty then kneed him in the gut and pinned him to the ground. She attempted to rip the bandana off his face, but the rider dislodged her hold.

Evan and the others sprayed the trees with a barrage of bullets. The bandits climbed back onto their horses and rode away.

Budd clutched his heaving chest as he struggled to catch his breath. "Get the stagecoach up!" he ordered. "We need to get out of here before they regroup."

"Anyone hurt?" Dotty asked.

"Steven was grazed, but we're all right," Evan replied. He yanked Leroy to his feet with a snarl and turned him over to Budd. "I got to fix the coach. You deal with him."

"Throwing off the coach was a good idea," Budd said to Leroy. "It might have worked if those men hadn't been sent to kill you."

"They were sent to free me."

Budd shook his head. "Hate to ruin your day, pal, but those bandits weren't shooting at us. Looks like Ripley Eagleson has cut you loose."

Chapter 6

Folks waved at Rip as he passed them by. He greeted each one with his usual air of respectability. Though Budd Mansfield had the lawmen on his side, Rip knew the people of Sacramento still held him in high regard.

After all, he had carefully crafted his identity as Reginald Pearce to be a man of the people. Folks had been eager to believe the kindhearted Mr. Pearce over a stranger like Budd Mansfield.

A young boy ran up to Rip and held his hand out expectantly. Rip tossed the boy a coin with a smile on his face and sauntered along the sidewalk. He whistled happily, going about his day as if he hadn't paid Sal to kill Leroy Murphy just hours before.

It would have been a mistake if he allowed the outlaw to live. Especially since Rip had found out that Murphy talked to Mansfield for days. Now that was something the gang leader had never allowed.

In the world that Ripley Eagleson reigned over, talking to his enemies was a quick way to end up buried beneath the daisies. Still, Leroy had been a good bandit and an even better lock breaker. It was a shame to lose someone so useful.

He opened the door to the hotel and walked up to the front desk. Rip paid for a room for the night before he headed upstairs. His room was at the end of the corridor, between the bathing quarters and the back entrance.

He unlocked the door and removed his hat, placing it on the table beside the door. The room was small but nicely furnished. Rip sat on the edge of the bed and pulled his jacket off.

The sound of a gun cocking made him freeze.

Sheriff Dawson stood beside the wardrobe with his gun aimed at Rip's chest. "Ripley Eagleson, you're under arrest for murder."

Rip raised his hands in surrender. "I-I don't know what's gotten into you, Sheriff, but I assure you you've got the wrong man."

"The act ends now," Dawson said. "I must admit, though, you had us all fooled. But I found the telegraph operator's body, Rip. He had the message to the marshal's office that only you and I knew about."

"Look, it ain't what you think," Rip replied. "My qualms ain't with you or this city. All I want is to make Pratt and Dempcy pay for what they did to me and my family."

The sheriff looked conflicted. "What happened?"

"I stole some money," Rip explained. "Not a lot. Just enough to feed those who were depending on me. But Thayer and the others... they wouldn't take pity on me. They fired me and spread gossip around town that I was a thief. I couldn't find work anywhere. The company ruined me."

"That's no excuse, Eagleson. You killed folk."

Rip shook his head. "You don't understand. I ain't the criminal here. It's them! Because I didn't have any money, I couldn't buy my mother's medicine. She died, sheriff. The sickness took her away from us, and I was left alone to care for Beatrice."

"Killing is never the answer," argued the lawman.

"I had to make money somehow," he continued, ignoring the sheriff's words. "Robbing those who robbed me seemed the only way I could make it. Ripley Eagleson had to disappear so Reginald Pearce could give his family what they deserved."

"What about the other families? What about the people who died—"

"What about me?" Rip shouted. "Nobody ever cared what happened to me! I don't deserve the ridicule and the blame. You especially should be concerned. After all, you wouldn't be sheriff right now if it hadn't been for me."

"I'm sheriff, because these good people put their faith in me."

"You're sheriff, because I told the mayor to pin a badge to your chest," he claimed. "No one in this godforsaken city would be anything without me. I helped to build this place up from the ground, and I'll be dead before I see it in the hands of you and Budd Mansfield!"

"The city belongs to the people. Not you, not me, and not Mansfield."

"Say what you will about me, but I've done nothing to anybody who didn't deserve it," Rip snapped. He stood up and ran his fingers through his hair. Pomade covered his hand, and he wiped it onto his pants.

"You killed the telegraph operator. He was an innocent man." Dawson dug for his cuffs, keeping his eyes on Rip the whole time. "You're responsible for all the people your men have killed. You're responsible for John Pepper's death and the death of all his victims. It's time to repent, Rip."

"Maybe you're right, Sheriff. Maybe I am responsible, but I would do it all over again if they gave me the chance." Rip acted fast.

He whipped his revolver out of the holster with the speed of a trained gunslinger and fired.

Sheriff Dawson spun before he hit the floor. There was a commotion down the hall. Rip abandoned everything and ran for the back entrance.

He lunged over the banister and muddy ground below. A man led his horse over to the public corral. Rip struck the man hard and fast before he hoisted himself into the saddle. Voices called out behind him as he raced out of Sacramento.

A plume of dust followed the horse as Rip spurred the poor creature on. They dashed over the flat desert land and over dry grass until reaching the forest.

Never once had Rip ridden so hard in his life. But when realization dawned that he had possibly killed the sheriff, panic overcame him.

There was nowhere left to hide, so Rip took the secret path to the Old Mill. It took him nearly two days to reach the hideout.

"Get ready!" he shouted when he arrived. "We move out now!"

***

Reno, Nevada

Budd signed the last of the documents the secretary of the mayor of Reno had given him. He sighed heavily before he handed them back.

Leroy Murphy was officially no longer his problem. It was as if they had lifted an enormous weight from his shoulders. "Thank you, ma'am," Budd said as he took his leave. "You have a good day now." The door closed softly behind him.

Reno was the only place near Sacramento where a judge was willing to go against the Blood Eagle Gang. Ripley Eagleson's name was like a shroud of shadow that hovered over the territory, striking fear into the hearts of many.

Budd would have been impressed if not for the Royal Hearts. Theodore Valentine's gang protected Reno and the surrounding settlements.

It was clear in the way Dotty walked around the city, as if she owned it. In some ways, she did.

Still, Budd headed over to the hotel, where he purchased two rooms for the night. Blake, Evan, and Steven were upset they had to bunk with Budd and his snoring, but none of them argued against the fact Dotty needed her own sleeping quarters. Money was tight between the four of them.

The sum of damages from the stagecoach robberies had come directly out of their pay. Budd saw it as more than fair, seeing as they had failed to protect Pratt & Dempcy's assets. He wandered into his room and saw only Steven remained.

"The others went to get supplies for the ride back to Sacramento," Steven said.

Budd replied with a simple nod. He watched Steven struggle to wrap his arm with bandages, but the man was too stubborn to give up. Budd swatted his hand away and took the cotton strips from the table.

He wiped the sweat from his brow and looked down at the wound on his friend's arm. Though it was clear to Budd the bandits hadn't been aiming for them, he still thought they had gotten lucky no one had been severely hurt in the scuffle.

Dotty had held her own, and so had the others. He placed his trust in them, and they proved their worth time and time again.

The wound looked as though it had at least been cleaned, which Budd saw as a miracle. There were few left in the world as bullheaded as the Wright brothers. He was careful not to wrap the bandages too tight around Steven's arm. "You and your brother have come a long way," Budd muttered. "Seems the days of you being an outlaw are over."

"I wish we had met you sooner. Budd, I will never forget you took a chance on us."

"I'm just glad I could help."

"It may have been Charles on the road," Steven said suddenly. "I can't count how many times we've fired at one another since all this started."

"You could have walked away at any point."

Steven shrugged. "Maybe. Or maybe I have to do this as much as you do."

"Family means everything," Budd said. "Whether or not you believe it now, you still love Charles. And when the time comes for you to choose between him and the rest of the world... your answer might just surprise you."

There was doubt in Steven's eyes even as he shook his head. "He's a killer, Budd. In more ways than you know. I've made peace with being the one to put an end to him so that Blake doesn't have to."

"That's… admirable."

"You don't talk about family much," said Steven. "Where's yours?"

Budd winced. He had pushed the past so far out of his mind. "I was an orphan. Made a few friends, and they became my family. Time got away from us, and we grew apart. Suddenly, I was on the outside of things again."

"Sounds rough."

"Not as much as you would think," Budd answered. "I've been blessed a few times in my life. When one family left me, the Lord gave me a new one. You, Blake, Evan, and Dotty… you all are my family now. Lord knows we'd all take a bullet for each other."

"I never took you for a religious man." Steven narrowed his eyes at Budd. "Never even heard you talk like this before."

Budd placed his hands flat on the table. The scars and calluses were a testament to how they had been used for violence most of his life. "I never was. But after the waterfall and getting pinned down by gunfire in the canyon, I figured someone was out there looking over me. Faith found me the day Dotty saved my life."

"I envy you," Steven said. "There's been a lot of darkness in the world that I can't ignore. Faith… keeps slipping through my fingers."

The door to the hotel room opened. Dotty and the others brought a few things inside. Evan set down some trays of food, Blake put some fresh clothes on the bed, and Dotty handed Budd a note.

He looked down at it in confusion. Eddie Goldman, a man Budd never expected to hear from so far west had written the note.

Budd hadn't seen Eddie in over three years. But if the detective was reaching out to Budd, that meant Eddie intended to get involved in the fight against Ripley Eagleson. Which was bad news for everyone.

Budd hopped out of his chair and walked over to Dotty. "The man who gave you this. Where is he?"

"He stopped me near the general store," she answered. "Said he was on his way out of town, but that you should expect him in Sacramento in a few weeks. Seemed like a nice man, all things considered. We could use some kindness after the day we've had."

"That man," Budd began. "That man ain't nice, Dotty. He'd have told a judge to give you the rope if he had known who you were. Eddie Goldman works for the Pinkertons." Realization then struck Budd that he stood in a hotel room surrounded by former outlaws, three of which were still wanted in several territories.

Chapter 7

The Old Mill

Rip left the stolen horse in the stables. He stormed off without a word and made his way inside. When he busted through the door, Hector and the others were seated around a table with cards in their hands. Rip grabbed Sal by the shirt and roughly jerked him out of the chair. "On your feet! Now!" he shouted. "Plans have changed, boys."

Sal shrugged off Rip's hold and stood in front of him defiantly. "The rest of the men have not arrived yet."

"I say we leave now, and that's exactly what you're going to do," Rip snapped. He slammed his gun onto the table with trembling hands. "Sheriff Dawson is dead. Now is the time to strike."

Charles smiled wickedly and clapped Sal on the arm. "We'll ride ahead and keep the deputies busy. Have fun, fellers. I know I will." Charles and Sal then hurried out of the building.

Pete and Hector remained by Rip's side as he geared up for the attack. Once he was swathed in black from head to foot, he stepped out into the light of day and whistled for his steed. Storm galloped out of the stables. The wild stallion tossed its mane and nudged Rip. "There you are. Miss me?"

He remembered the day he first laid eyes on Storm. The horse had been an untamed beast back then, roaming the grasslands. Rip had walked right up to Storm and saw the anger and wildness in his gaze. The two had been practically inseparable since. Storm bucked anyone out of the saddle who wasn't Rip.

"This might be our last ride, old friend," he whispered to the mount. "You just stay out of the way when the shooting starts."

Storm lipped at Rip's hand as if to reassure his rider.

Rip stuck his foot in the stirrups and hoisted himself into the saddle. He settled easily and rode over to the camp. The bell chimed loudly upon his approach. Men gathered nearby. Rip looked down into the faces of each and every one of them. "I don't know how your bosses ran their operations," he started. "But I run things strictly around here."

There were a few grumbles in response.

"You shoot no one who isn't aiming to shoot you. Women and children are to remain unharmed. Take what you can carry and nothing more," he stated. "Charles, Salazar, Hector, and Pete are your leaders. In my absence, you follow their orders. Now, anybody who has a problem with those rules… will be dealt with in a manner I deem fit. Any questions?"

There were only a few more grumbles and barely audible words of agreement. After Rip finished his speech, the group dispersed. Several outlaws readied their weapons, while others prepared the horses. There were just under twenty bandits in total, a number that had shocked even Rip. His allies seemed eager to see him send a message to the law—a message that the west still belonged to the outcasts.

Storm took the lead as a horde of outlaws rode out of the Old Mill. Through the rough forest terrain, across hills and valleys, and over vast desert landscapes they went. Rip stopped his men on the outskirts of Black Lake. Smoke filled the sky as Charles and Sal ravaged the little town. Several buildings had been set ablaze in the chaos. Rip closed his eyes and listened to the screams.

"Pete, take half the men into Black Lake," he ordered. "The rest will follow me and Hector to Sacramento. When Mansfield arrives, hold him off for a while before you three join us again."

"Got it, boss."

Though his words had been nothing but agreeable, Rip heard something off in Pete's voice. The youngest member of his gang seemed far too nervous for Rip's comfort. There were twenty saddle-raw, hungry bandits who waited to raid a few towns. It was not the time for Pete to get nervous. "Speak up now," he growled.

"This just ain't our way of doin' things."

"Our way of doing things is whatever I say it is. Now is not the time to question me," Rip barked. He turned Storm so he faced Pete. "This is my gang, and these men follow my command. Go down there and show them what the Blood Eagles are capable of. And if you have a problem with that, I would be happy to beat that cowardice out of you, boy."

Ripples of heat permeated up from the ground. Sweat poured down Rip's face, trailing down the bridge of his nose before it soaked into the scarf that concealed his identity. Roiling pillars of blackened smoke floated up toward the unrelenting sun. Rip watched Pete with a narrowed gaze.

The young man broke off from the group and led nearly a dozen bandits further into Black Lake.

Charles's shout of victory was heard above the cries of panic. Rip smiled beneath his mask and clucked his tongue. Storm slowly turned in the direction of Sacramento. They rode for hours, marking the roads with a stampede of hooves. Hector and his mare stayed close to Rip and Storm as they drew closer to their mark.

Once they reached the outskirts of the city, Rip dug for his gun and fired three warning shots into the air. Heads turned in his direction as a burning whiskey bottle soared over his head. A woman's scream sent the town into a fit of hysterics. Still, that wicked grin never wavered beneath the black cotton scarf. "Charge!" He shouted above the chaos, and a swarm of outlaws dashed toward Sacramento.

***

Black Lake, California

Budd woke the following morning, greeted by gray skies as the sun slowly rose in the distance. He tossed a boot at Evan. The young deputy bolted upright and shot Budd a murderous glare. Evan then shook Steven and Blake until they woke. Four pairs of tired eyes blinked around the room. Budd climbed out of the bed with a yawn and stretched high above his head.

"Time to get going," Budd grumbled sleepily. "We have less than a day to make it to Black Lake."

The others muttered foul curses under their breath as Budd got to it. He washed up with a rag, using the water basin before he cleaned his teeth. Breakfast was a dry biscuit and a lump of cold bacon he had wrapped up in his satchel. After he changed into fresh clothes, Budd plucked up the courage to go wake Dotty. Only Budd and the good Lord knew just how nervous he was.

He entered the corridor quietly and approached the door to her room. A soft knock echoed down the hall. Dotty opened the door with a scowl. "It's barely dawn, Budd Mansfield. I suggest you have a good reason for waking me so early."

"Be ready in an hour," he said.

But one hour had turned into two as Budd waited with the stagecoach while the others prepared for the journey ahead. He glanced down at his pocket watch and hissed through his teeth. There was only another half hour before the window of opportunity closed and they were stuck in the city until the next day. If they weren't out of Reno by then, Budd would have been forced to escort a transport. Working for Pratt & Dempcy was a demanding job.

Luckily, Budd's companions exited the hotel a few seconds later. He spared them a speech about being punctual, but he made sure to give them all pointed looks. Dotty at least had the decency to pretend she was ashamed. Budd took her hand and helped her up onto the bench seat of the stagecoach. The blush upon her cheeks deepened to a darker shade of red as she avoided his gaze.

"Thank you," Dotty murmured.

"It was no problem at all." Budd cleared his throat and looked around uncomfortably. He tucked a wayward lock of hair behind his ear as he circled around to the other side of the coach. His gun clanked against the bench as he situated himself on the seat.

Something seemed to have changed between them. The awareness that pulled them together had grown into more since Dotty's confession. And Budd suspected Theodore Valentine had been correct in assuming Budd had feelings for Dotty. There was no denying she was an incredible woman, one Budd would have been lucky to call his own. However, there were more pressing matters that needed his attention. Thoughts of courtship and romantic feelings were set aside as his mind turned to recent events.

Time moved slowly as the others filled the stagecoach with provisions. It was a long ride ahead of them. Budd hated the idea of not making it to Black Lake in time and being forced to camp in the valley for the night. Not that he disliked being out in the wilderness. Being punctual was just something he prided himself on. Besides, there was no telling when Ripley Eagleson's gang might attack. So Budd and Dotty rode up front. Blake, Evan, and Steven flanked the stagecoach with their horses.

Off they went.

The constant rattle of the stagecoach was soothing as they ventured over the sprawling landscapes of Nevada. But the scent of pine was strong as they reached the forest that lay between Reno and Sacramento. Dark, thick patches of trees peppered the mountainous terrain. Budd kept his sharp gaze on the tree line, searching for any sign of attack.

"Keep moving," he said quietly. "We can't slow down just yet."

The sun moved across the sky as the hours passed and they crept closer to town. A hawk shrieked overhead before it swooped through the treetops. Streaks of colors painted the clouds as the day turned to night. Stars appeared like flickering lanterns against an ocean of darkness. The forest disappeared behind them, fading into the distance, while the rooftops of Black Lake came into view.

"Wait…" Dotty's voice cracked. She lifted her finger, pointing to a smokestack above the town. "Something is wrong. We need to hurry!"

Budd cracked the reins, and the horses shot off toward Black Lake. "Ride ahead and see what's going on!" he shouted to Steven. He watched as the former outlaw spurred his horse on, passing the stagecoach. Amber light washed over the town as flames moved across the buildings.

"The whole town is on fire. I can hear the screams," Evan said. "Budd, Sacramento might be in trouble too…"

Budd turned to Dotty. He opened his mouth to speak, but no words left his lips. She seemed to understand what he needed before he said anything. "I'll go. Don't worry about me. Be safe, Budd." Dotty leaped onto the back of Evan's horse. The mount sprinted into the night, leaving behind a cloud of dust that hovered in the air.

The stagecoach jostled as the horses raced down Calligan Road. Budd pulled it to a stop at the edge of town and hopped down from the bench. He spotted a man nearby, frozen with shock as the town burned. "Get some water on those flames!" he said to the man—which woke him from his daze. The man hurried to do as Budd asked. Folks gathered to throw dirt, water, and anything else they could think of to snuff out the flames. Budd ran over to the town well and hoisted the bucket out of its depths. "I need some help over here!"

Chapter 8

Hooves pounded against the road, kicking up dirt as Dotty and Evan rode toward Sacramento. Dotty heard gunshots over the sound of her pounding heart.

There was no smoke or crackling flames as they approached, only shouts of alarm that rang into the night. Evan's horse bucked and nearly knocked Dotty off its back, but she held on with all her strength.

"Over there!" she shouted as she pointed to a group of deputies trying to hold off the bandits. "They look like they could use our help."

Evan gave a curt nod and turned toward the lawmen.

Dotty didn't wait for the horse to stop before she jumped off. She landed hard on the ground and rolled, coming to a crouch beside the crumbling wall where the deputies took shelter. They eyed her suspiciously.

Dotty lifted her skirt and pulled a knife from her boot. She launched it at the nearest bandit, hitting him square in the chest. "Eyes on the fight, boys! They're pushing forward."

"Who are you?" one of them asked.

"The name is Dorothy Valentine, but you can call me Dotty." She flipped her sidearm out of its holster and grabbed her second pistol. Dotty fired both weapons at the bandits, sending them running for cover. "Where's the sheriff?"

"Sheriff Dawson was shot three days ago by Ripley Eagleson. He's in the infirmary."

Dotty's blood turned cold. "Who's the sheriff now?"

"W-we don't got one."

The men looked at one another with uncertainty, and she rolled her eyes. "Don't all volunteer at once now," she scoffed irritably. "And the mayor?"

"We've got four deputies guardin' the mayor's house, but the outlaws are relentless," said one of the lawmen. "The marshal hasn't arrived yet, and we're runnin' out of bullets."

Dotty thought of a plan. She took a deep breath and vaulted over the crumbling wall. Bullets flew past her head as she sprinted for the bank.

Dotty shot one outlaw and then another, but bandits turned on her left and right. She fired blindly until she was out of rounds and holstered her guns.

Her hand touched the bank doors just as an explosion sent her catapulting backward. Dust and debris rained down upon Dotty as she struggled to breathe. Black spots danced in her vision.

"We got the vault open!" a voice cried triumphantly.

Dotty barely heard a thing over the sound of the ringing in her ears. She slowly climbed to her feet and limped over to the wall of the bank.

Her boots crunched on piles of glass that littered the ground as she snuck up behind one of the bandits. She pressed the muzzle of her gun to the back of his head. "Hand me your gun. Nice and slow," Dotty said with a low voice, trying her best to imitate a man's.

The bandit held his shotgun out to the side.

She snatched it with her free hand. "Now get on your knees and don't say a word."

When the outlaw followed her orders, Dotty used the shotgun to knock him unconscious. The man slumped over the charred remnants of the front counter of the bank.

Once she was sure he was out cold, Dotty waved over the other deputies. They followed her into the back, where three other bandits stuffed handfuls of cash and banknotes into bags.

Dotty counted down from five before she charged the nearest bandit. Startled by her sudden appearance, the man dropped the bag of money and fumbled with his gun.

Dotty managed to cock the shotgun and lift it before he got a shot off. The deputies held the other two bandits at gunpoint.

But something wasn't quite right about all this. Black Lake had been nearly burned to the ground for a bank robbery? No, none of it made sense. Why had the bandits attacked both towns? Why had they targeted the bank and the mayor's office in Sacramento but not in Black Lake?

Dotty wondered if it had all been a ruse—a distraction for something far more sinister. Then again, there was the possibility Ripley Eagleson was behind it all. She wiped the sweat from her brow as she pondered and gestured for the bandit to drop to his knees.

"How many of you are there?" Dotty asked.

The bandit said nothing.

She reached forward and yanked the mask off his face. "Archer White," Dotty sneered. "I thought you'd be in the ground by now. Guess it was just wishful thinking on my part that the world was rid of another yellow-bellied coward."

"You look good, Dotty."

"Tell me, are you working for the Blood Eagles?" she asked, ignoring the lecherous gaze he threw her way. "Did Ripley put you up to this?"

Archer went quiet again, confirming Dotty's suspicions. She limped closer to the outlaw and tapped his shoulder with the shotgun. "You know me, Archer White. If you stay silent, I might just take offense, and that... that ain't good news for you." Dotty met the outlaw's stare. She let the threat of her words sink in and asked again. "Did Ripley Eagleson order you to attack Sacramento?"

"He did," Archer replied. "But Eagleson don't care about money or reputation."

"What's he after?"

"What he's always been after," Archer snorted. "Pratt and Dempcy."

Dotty left Archer and the other outlaws in the capable hands of the deputies. She shuffled back outside, where a crowd had gathered to watch. Evan rushed to her side and helped her lean against one of the pillars outside the bank.

Her eyes wandered over to Pratt & Dempcy's office, but nothing seemed out of the ordinary. It was one of the only buildings along the road that hadn't been riddled with bullets.

"We need to protect the mayor," Evan said. "Those bandits are putting up one hell of a fight." He helped Dotty stand and threw her arm over his shoulder to support her weight as they walked. Already the sounds of fighting were heard echoing off the buildings.

***

Sacramento, California
A few hours later

Ripley Eagleson opened the door to Pratt & Dempcy's office. The young woman who worked at the front desk shrank back in fear. She lifted her arms to shield herself as Rip raised his gun.

He cocked the hammer back and lowered his voice to a deep drawl. "Get out of here," Rip growled. He flicked the gun toward the door and watched as the young woman ran outside as fast as she could.

The door closed with a quiet thud.

"Harriet?" called Howard Thayer from his office. "Put Mr. Thomas down for tomorrow afternoon. He wishes to go over his deposit before arranging for his daughter to visit from Philadelphia. Harriet?"

Rip nudged open the door and held his gun high. "Harriet ain't here."

Mr. Thayer dropped the papers in his hand. They fluttered to the floor slowly as the man stood and trembled with fear. "W-who are you?" he asked, voice cracking as if the words had been forced out. "There's no money here."

Rip chuckled. He pulled the scarf down from his face, revealing his identity to Mr. Thayer. Realization appeared in the man's gaze, and a swell of satisfaction welled inside of Rip.

He watched as that realization turned to terror, wondering to himself if the man felt as guilty as he looked. "You took everything from me," Rip said. "And now I'm here to take everything from you. Pratt and Dempcy will never send another stagecoach through my territory again, and that is a promise."

"Ripley Eagleson."

"Have a seat, Howard," Rip ordered while gesturing to the chair. Once the manager of the stagecoach company sat down, Rip took a seat across from the desk. He propped his feet up and kept the gun leveled on Mr. Thayer. "Now, I want you to apologize."

Howard Thayer shook his head slowly. "You must let the past rest, Ripley."

"It may be the past for you, but I'm the one who must live with—"

"Yourself," Mr. Thayer interrupted. "You have to live with yourself."

"I was innocent!"

"You were a thief."

"I stole only to provide for my family," Rip shouted. "I had a sick mother and a little sister to look after! I was young and naive, but I was never a criminal."

Thayer shook his head once again. "You never could see the truth."

"So, help me see." Rip clenched his jaw tightly, flexing the muscle until it ached. "Tell me what I did that was so wrong. Tell me what I did to deserve shame and ridicule."

"I tried to help you, to give you a chance to come clean and return the money."

Rip stood up. The chair toppled over. "You ruined me!" he shrieked. Rip paced in front of the desk, waving the gun wildly as he spoke. "Everyone in town spat in my face. The company abandoned me. I was thrown in jail like an animal and beaten by the lawmen who were supposed to be a symbol of justice and order. My mother died, and I wasn't there to bury her. My sister was left alone to fend for herself… a young girl drowning in a sea of viciousness. Forced to work her fingers to the bone and marry men like John Pepper." The name had been growled with such hatred that it shocked even him.

"I'm sorry all of that came to pass, but you can't simply blame the company."

"Pratt and Dempcy should have done more," Rip claimed. "They should have worried more for their workers and their families than the rich city folk they doted on. And so, I made things right. I set the balance."

"You became a killer."

"No," he replied. "I became an angel of vengeance—the right hand of truth and justice. I provided for my men and their loved ones the way Pratt and Dempcy had never done for me!"

The lies slid from his tongue as easily as they always had. Rip had even started to believe them himself, believe he was some image of all that was good and benevolent. It was anything but true, for a black heart beat strongly in his chest.

"You don't have to do this…"

"Yes, I do," Rip said. "Ripley Eagleson and Reginald Pearce will die with Sacramento. They will die with Pratt and Dempcy. And from the ashes of this godforsaken city, a new redeemer will rise. People will turn to me for safety. They'll turn to me for fortune and prosperity." Rip squeezed the trigger.

The bullet hit the back of Mr. Thayer's chair as the man dove out of the way. Shards of wood sprayed the wall as a second hole was punched through the chair by another bullet.

Mr. Thayer crawled across the floor and reached for the edge of the window. Rip cocked his pistol and fired a third time, hitting the hand that attempted to open the shutters for an escape.

He heard Thayer's startled cry. Blood dripped onto the floorboards. Rip stood over his former employer as if he were a predator stalking its prey. His icy gaze sparkled with joy at the sight of such potent fear.

"Please," Mr. Thayer begged. "I have a family. Th-they won't know what to do without me. My daughter..."

"That's right," Rip snarled. "Beg like I begged for you to help me. Beg like the pathetic swine you are!" He raised his gun again, ready to end it all.

"Where the hell are you, Eagleson?"

The door was knocked off its hinges, crashing to the floor with a loud bang. Blake Wright stood in the doorway with a rifle aimed at Rip. But the outlaw was too quick. He tackled Blake to the ground and bashed him in the face with the end of his pistol. Blake brought his knee up and rammed it into Rip's side. The rifle slid across the floor, landing right at Howard Thayer's feet.

Chapter 9

Black Lake, California

Budd Mansfield tossed a bucket of water onto yet another fire. Smoke and steam puffed up toward his face. He pulled the bandana from his back pocket and held it over his mouth and nose.

Someone nearby shouted there was a child trapped inside one of the burning houses. Budd dropped the bucket and jumped into action.

Fire licked at his boots as he leapt over the flames. The house gave a warbling groan as the walls caved. Budd coughed into the bandana and searched for the missing child.

Tears streamed down his face as the smoke burned his eyes. Sweat mixed with soot, painting his skin as black as tar. "Call out to me!" he shouted. "Anybody in here?"

Budd stopped and listened. He heard a faint voice just as the beam over his head snapped. Charred wood fell all around, blocking his path. A rush of heat engulfed his arm, and he saw his sleeve had caught fire.

Budd slapped out the flames before they burned his skin. It riddled his jacket with holes.

"Over here!" squeaked a small voice.

Through the smoke and embers, Budd saw a tiny form huddled in the corner. He carefully climbed over the fallen beam. Each step caused the floorboards to shift dangerously beneath his weight.

He reached out a blackened hand toward the child. Impossibly small hands wrapped around his fingers. Budd gave a yank, pulling the child against the safety of his chest. The floor caved in beneath them.

Down they fell to the first level of the house.

Budd tucked the child closer to his body and took the brunt of the fall on his back. Tears wet his shirt as he sucked in a lung full of smoke. Budd scrambled for the bandana and covered the child's mouth.

He crawled across the floor with his free hand, scooting closer and closer to freedom. "Keep your head down," Budd croaked. "We're almost there."

They reached the front door of the house. Steven Wright splashed a bucket of water over them the second they broke free. Budd handed the child off and clawed at the collar of his shirt until the buttons tore off. He coughed roughly, dragging in mouthfuls of air until he finally breathed normally. His vision cleared as the sun rose over Black Lake.

"You're a madman," Steven said as he helped Budd to his feet. "What were you thinkin' runnin' into a fire like that?"

"Is the kid all right?"

"He'll live," said Steven irritably. But there was no actual anger in his voice. "You just can't help being a hero, can you?"

"I was just doing what anyone would have done." Budd splashed water on his face, surprised steam hadn't risen from his skin. "Any word from Sacramento?"

Steven shook his head. "The fires are out, and the bandits ran out of town."

"Which direction?" Budd asked. The silence that followed his question was like a slug to the chest. He knew the bandits had moved on to Sacramento, that the attack had only just begun.

Deep inside, Budd blamed himself. He could have prevented all the destruction had he been willing to believe Reginald Pearce and Ripley Eagleson were the same man. The blame was his alone.

"We need to get to Sacramento before the bandits arrive," Budd said. "You know a shortcut?"

"Faster than Calligan Road?" Blake asked as he scratched his head. "Maybe. But you ain't gonna like it. We got to cut through the river and follow it straight into the city."

"Then we ride immediately." Budd hobbled over to the stagecoach, where Ivory waited. He shoved his foot into the stirrups and pushed off the ground, throwing himself into the saddle.

Ivory shuffled in place. Budd awkwardly adjusted his balance before urging his horse forward. He met Steven near the stables.

They cut across farms and plots of land covered in dry, frail grass. The sun was high in the sky by the time they reached the river. It slashed through the landscape, connecting towns and settlements for miles upon miles.

Budd and Steven rode through the river and along the bank. The men felt miserable in singed, dampened clothes as they trudged through the muck. The horses kicked up mud, sand, and clumps of grass.

But it was less than a half day's ride before they reached Sacramento. And, though there were no fires, sounds of war were all around.

Budd half expected to find Gatling guns and cannons lingering in the streets of the city. Gunfire drew them toward the mayor's office, where a shootout had been underway between the Blood Eagle Gang and the lawmen of Sacramento.

Budd cursed loudly as the other bandits arrived on their horses.

"Over here!" Dotty's head popped up from behind a broken window. She fired a rifle with ease, spraying the ground near the bandits with bullets. The horses were spooked.

Several mounts bucked their riders and ran off behind the buildings. But the bandits returned fire. They fought with a vengeance.

The fight raged on as Budd climbed down from Ivory's back. Out of the corner of his eye, Budd spotted a group of outlaws escaping with bags of loot. They overran the entire city. Budd knew he had to even the odds.

He grabbed his rifle and secondary sidearm from the saddle bag. He then gave his horse a swat on the rear and sent her off to safety.

Dotty, Blake, Evan, and the deputies had fought hard to defend the mayor's office. They barricaded the entrance and set up guards everywhere. Budd was impressed by the level of dedication they showed.

But the sight of a battered Blake Wright hadn't escaped his notice. "What happened?" Budd asked. "Looks like you took on a badger."

"Ripley Eagleson." Blake pointed to where a group of outlaws surrounded the Pratt & Dempcy office. "Salazar Torez showed up and hit me from behind. I got Mr. Thayer out, but the gang is working on the safe and the strongboxes in the back right now."

***

Sweat burned her eyes. Dotty tore off her bonnet and tossed it aside as she adjusted her aim. Her hands were steady when she pulled the trigger

Down went another outlaw. She flipped the lever, ejecting the case before she cocked the hammer again. The second shot hit its mark, and another bandit dropped to the dirt.

Dotty stared down her sights and spotted Budd as he approached. She pushed all thoughts of him out of her mind and concentrated on the fight.

"Here they come, boys!" Dotty shouted. "Get ready!"

The bandits attempted another charge just as Dotty's rifle jammed. Black powder covered her hands as she fumbled to fix it. "Hold them off for me. I'll be ready in a minute." Luckily, Dotty's father's obsession with guns meant she knew what to do in these moments.

Once everything was in place, Dotty smacked her palm against the side of the rifle and smiled. She took aim once more and then fired.

"Get Valentine!" one bandit yelled.

A barrage of bullets came her way.

Dotty ducked down from the broken window. She curled herself into a ball and breathed deeply through her mouth to keep from breathing in too much dirt from the debris.

White-hot pain caused her to clench her teeth as a bullet grazed her arm. She looked down at the blood that stained the sleeve of her dress and cursed in a very unladylike manner.

Dotty pressed her back to the wall and ripped her sleeve down. She used the scrap of cloth to tie off the wound to keep it from bleeding too much.

When there was a break in the gunfire, Dotty reloaded her rifle and snuck outside. She came around the corner and threw herself into Budd's arms.

He hissed in pain and Dotty panicked. She checked him from head to boot in search of injuries. There were some bruises forming on his torso and a large cut on his hip. "I'm tiring of nursing you back to health, Budd Mansfield," she teased with a smile. It thrilled Dotty, he had made it back to her.

Though Budd returned her smile, it was obvious to Dotty that something heavy weighed on his mind. "The fires were terrible, Dotty. It'll take a long time before Black Lake can heal from something like this... It may just be the end."

"There's still hope for them here in Sacramento. We just need to keep fighting." Dotty left Budd with the others and made her way to the back of the mayor's office. She crept along the wall and slid open a window before she climbed inside.

Her foot touched the floor as a man's shadow engulfed her. Dotty readied herself to scream, but a hand clamped over her mouth before she made a sound.

Mayor Thomas.

Dotty breathed a sigh of relief when he lowered his hand. "You frightened me," she whispered harshly. "I'm here to protect you, Mr. Mayor."

The man looked skeptical until she reached back through the window and fetched the rifle. "You must be the infamous Miss Valentine I've been hearin' so much about," he said. "I'll thank you for defending me and my city, but I don't want none of your trouble around here when this is over."

Dotty felt a twinge of anger at the mayor's remarks. "Yes, sir. You won't have to worry about me. Though I must admit I'm disappointed, you allowed Ripley Eagleson to make things this bad. People are dying, Mayor, and you have some of the blame to share."

"Now, see here—"

Gunfire resumed outside.

Dotty shoved the mayor behind his desk. She unlocked the door to allow the others inside for better cover.

Instead of fighting beside his men, the mayor had cowered in his office. The whole thing made Dotty feel repulsed by the man.

She sneered at him as Blake, Evan, Budd, and Steven helped the injured deputies inside.

Dotty then got to work stripping lines of fabric from her dress to wrap their wounds. "Hold still," she said. "This may smart a bit."

Budd stood over her as she forced a man's broken arm back into place. His screams reverberated off the walls and caused her ears to ring. More cries of pain were heard before she was finished, though. Many of the deputies had been hurt in the fight as they struggled to defend the city.

Dotty tried her best to tend to each one of them, although they would have thrown her in a cell under different circumstances.

"Where's Eagleson now?" Budd asked.

Dotty chewed her lip in thought. "Pratt and Dempcy's was the last Blake saw of him. Coward most likely ran once the fighting got worse." She gestured toward the roof of the bank where Hector Vasquez had taken up the post. "They got a sharpshooter on the roof. Salazar Torez and Charles Wright are still at Mr. Thayer's office. I ain't too sure where Pete Jones is, either."

"We saw Jones riding this way with more bandits. They arrived just as we did." Budd helped barricade the front. Bookshelves were toppled over onto their sides to block all the windows, but one, and the mayor's desk had been pushed in front of the door.

"Evan, head to the bank and take out Hector. Dotty, you stay here with Steven and protect Mayor Thomas. Blake is coming with me to Pratt and Dempcy's."

Dotty readied her weapons and climbed back through the window. She slung the rifle over her shoulder by the strap, took the ladder up to the roof, and hunkered down behind a short wall. Her leg hurt and the wound on her arm still burned, but Dotty was ready to fight until the end.

She watched as Evan exited the mayor's office. The sly deputy cut through the alleyways, avoiding the direct fight. Budd and Steven left after Evan. And Dotty watched their backs from the roof.

Chapter 10

"Go check around back for footprints," Budd ordered Blake. They had to find Ripley Eagleson.

Someone had to pay for what they had done to Black Lake and Sacramento. And though he had more answers to his questions, Budd needed solutions—solutions he hoped ended with Ripley Eagleson facing the hangman's noose. There was no place in the world for his sort of evil.

Budd pushed open the door to Howard Thayer's office. They had picked the safe clean, along with the strongboxes. He walked past the safe and over to the desk, where papers sat askew.

Bullet holes riddled the wall behind the desk, a broken chair leaned against the wall, and scuff marks marred the floor. Budd thought Blake and Ripley Eagleson must have had a messy brawl.

Floorboards behind Budd squeaked.

"Well, well, well," said a masked bandit. "Look what we've got here."

There was a second bandit who walked into the room as well. "Bless my stars," the second bandit snorted. "If it ain't Budd Mansfield himself."

The bandit removed his mask, and his partner did the same. Bud recognized them. He had known them in a life that seemed like it had faded away.

He had fought these men, hogtied them, and handed them over to the Pinkertons back when he thought he had something to prove to the world.

"Tyler Cooper and Josiah Hersley," Budd breathed in surprise. "This is a long way from Texas. What brings you boys this far west?"

"Ripley Eagleson promised more money than we can ever spend," Josiah chuckled. "And the satisfaction of seein' you grovel on your knees, of course."

"Well, Ripley Eagleson might be known for his generosity toward the folks he robs, but he ain't too kind to criminals. Did you ask him what happened to Leroy Murphy?"

Tyler and Josiah looked at one another for a moment. "Leroy was rescued," Josiah said. "Rip told us all about how you tried to get Leroy to turn."

"No, Rip sent a group of men to kill Leroy the second he was being transferred to Reno," Budd explained. "They attacked us in the forest, but they were only aiming for him. That's what Ripley Eagleson does to those he calls family."

Tyler and Josiah looked at one another in confusion. Josiah stepped toward Budd and, in the blink of an eye, the three of them had their guns drawn. It was a standoff. Tyler and Josiah each had a pistol drawn, but Budd had two. His arms ached from the effort it took to hold up his sidearm and secondary weapon. The fall he took in the burning building must have taken more out of him than he thought.

Tyler cocked his pistol and gave Budd a sidelong glare. "You always were a liar, Budd Mansfield. Rip's gang is his family. And he always takes care of family."

"He'll hang you out to dry as soon as he sees a chance," Budd said. "And when he does, I want you to look back on this moment and remember that things could have been different."

He looked to the doorway and saw a shadow. Blake appeared behind the bandits with his gun drawn. The former outlaw shuffled closer to Tyler and Josiah, moving quietly in a way that made Budd think of a sly mountain lion.

"Drop your guns," Blake ordered. "And slide them across the floor."

Tyler and Josiah audibly gasped. Josiah's hand trembled, but he kept his gun aimed at Budd. Tyler spun around quickly and knocked Blake's gun aside.

Blake tackled the bandit into the wall. A painting fell to the floor just as Josiah lunged for Budd. The moment of surprise was gone.

Budd kicked Josiah in the chest, sending the outlaw flying toward the wall. Plaster cracked and crumbled upon impact. Josiah scrambled for his dropped gun, but Budd was on him in an instant.

They kicked the gun to the other side of the room. Josiah was held at gunpoint once again, unarmed and out of options.

Budd glanced over his shoulder to where Blake had Tyler in a similar predicament. Both bandits submitted with their hands raised high.

It was a small victory. One overshadowed by the joy Budd felt when the gunfire outside finally ended. He heard a stampede of horses retreat and closed his eyes for just a moment of peace.

Though it wasn't much in the aftermath of such destruction, Budd was thankful when silence fell over Sacramento. He then removed his belt and used it to hogtie Josiah.

"Take care of his partner. I must go check on the mayor's office," Budd said. "Let's meet back at the jailhouse in an hour."

They shook hands before Budd dragged Josiah out of Mr. Thayer's office at Pratt & Dempcy. Out on the street, there were crowds of people gathered along the wooden planks of the sidewalk.

They gawked as Budd shoved Josiah over to the deputies. Among them were Evan and Steven. The two men shared a worried look before they approached Budd. Evan was the first who spoke.

"The fight is over but…" Evan began. "People from Black Lake are already flooding in. They need shelter, and we need to put together groups to look for bodies. It's a tough job, but with the sheriff hurt and now the mayor injured… I think that responsibility falls to the one they trust to fix all this. And that's you, Budd."

No mayor, no sheriff, and somehow Budd wound up in charge. Either his life was cursed or God had a sense of humor.

Either way, Budd had no choice but to comply. He formed one posse for searches and another for repairs. Everyone pulled their weight.

Folks came together to help one another. It was a beautiful sight to behold after a tragedy.

Despite Budd's efforts, Black Lake was gone—burned to the ground with nothing but blackened ruins left behind. The townspeople helped repair Sacramento, but there was a palpable loss that could be felt. It hovered over the city like a dark cloud.

Budd had even ridden back to the town hoping to find survivors or even something worth salvaging. There were a few people trapped in their homes, so he worked hard to free them.

Those who were willing to start over in the city rode back to Sacramento with Budd. Those who weren't... started their journey further west, hoping to find a new settlement.

Budd wished them the best in their ambitious endeavors. He arrived back in Sacramento a week later, eager to talk to his partners about housing situations.

However, when he entered the sheriff's office, he hadn't seen hope on the men's faces. Instead, there was an air of fear and anger. Evan stood up when Budd walked over the threshold.

"What's wrong?" Budd asked. "Was there another attack?"

"No," answered Evan. "We could recover our fallen and reunite a lot of folks with their loved ones. But no one has seen Dotty since they shot the mayor. Doc says he might not make it. He fears infection is inevitable."

"That's too bad. How's Sheriff Dawson?"

"Making a quick recovery," Evan sighed. "We're lucky Eagleson's aim was off. Another inch to the left, and Dawson would have been meeting the Lord a lot quicker than he intended."

"And Dotty?" Budd looked at Blake and Steven. The two had been practically silent and stone-faced since they learned their brother Charles was among the captured bandits.

Steven cleared his throat and shook his head. "No sign of Dotty outside of town, either. We've been helpin' with the searches, so there ain't been a lot of time to look into it. But she's a strong one. I'm sure she's all right."

"She ain't all right," said a voice from the cells. Charles Wright leaned against the bars and jangled his empty water cup. "I'm thirsty. Why don't you be a good dog and fetch me some water, and I'll tell you all about it."

"Tell me where she is." Budd stepped closer to the cell and yanked the cup out of the prisoner's hand. "And *maybe* I'll get you some water."

"*Where,* ain't so important," Charles chuckled. "It's *who* she's with that's the problem. My partner can be quite creative when he's mad. And Dorothy Valentine is one woman who ended up his enemy."

"You ain't giving me much." Budd dipped the cup into the water bucket. He then held it just out of reach of the bandit behind bars.

"Salazar Torez," Charles said.

A collection of gasps sounded in the room. Budd looked over at Steven and Blake Wright. The worry on their faces made him uneasy. Though Dotty had mentioned Torez a few times, Budd wasn't familiar with the bandit's work outside of what they had done in Ripley Eagleson's name.

If it had the Wright brothers worried, Budd figured he wouldn't like what Charles said next.

"Salazar is a man who specializes in cruelty. He's tortured folks so bad that they prayed for the reaper to come knockin'," Charles stated. "He took her. And he'll get her to hand over her father or else..."

"Or else?"

Charles made a gun gesture with his hand and pressed the tips of his fingers to his temple. "Defyin' Ripley Eagleson will be the last thing she does if Sal has anythin' to say about it."

Budd handed over the water cup and stormed out of the sheriff's office. He turned the corner, only to run into Sheriff Dawson himself. The lawman was pale in the face, and there were large bandages peeking out beneath the collar of his shirt.

But he was alive, which was all that mattered. Budd offered his arm, but it was clear Dawson's pride wouldn't let him accept any help. "Sheriff, good to see you on your feet."

"I wasn't going to lie in the infirmary after hearing the mayor had been shot," Dawson answered. "This city needs me, Mansfield."

"Well, I ain't gonna argue that," Budd said. "I can't be in three places at once. We could really use your expertise now that we have seven of Eagleson's men in the jailhouse and sheriff's office."

Dawson whistled. "Seven? That's a lot of bandits. I'm sorry I couldn't help fight. I hope my men served you well."

"They've earned their badges," Budd replied. "But I have something to take care of, sheriff. My men are in there with Evan. They'll be willing to help where they're needed."

"Appreciated. Much appreciated." Sheriff Dawson limped inside just as Budd made his way onto the sidewalk.

Budd waited until the lawman disappeared before he walked down to the hotel. He entered the lobby, unsurprised that they packed the entire room to the rafters with Black Lake folks looking for shelter. His eyes scanned the faces in the crowd.

He spotted Theodore Valentine's goon sitting in the corner with a cup of coffee clutched in his hand. Budd pulled the second chair from his table out and took a seat before the man could speak. "Where's your boss?" he asked. "And be quick. This is a serious situation."

"Mr. Valentine wishes to extend his apologies. He wishes not to involve himself in your affairs."

"To hell with that!" Budd slammed his fist onto the table. "Dotty's been kidnapped, and I need his help to find her."

Chapter 11

Somewhere in Yosemite Valley, California

The smell of rotted wood and mildew tinted the air, causing Dotty's nose to scrunch as she blinked open her eyes. Bright light filtered in through a large crack in the wall. The sun illuminated the contents of a small hovel.

A man slept in the corner with his back to her. Dotty flexed her fingers and felt the muscles in her arms ache. Ropes bound her limbs tight behind her back.

Face down on the floor, she had no hope of escaping. So, Dotty rolled onto her side and took in her surroundings. There was nothing in sight to free her arms. But Dotty pulled her knees toward her chest, curled into a ball, and used her fingers to loosen the ropes around her ankles. There was a twinge in her hip, but she freed her legs from the binds.

"Clever," a voice said from behind Dotty.

She stilled.

Salazar stepped into her line of sight and crouched down. He picked up the rope that had been around her ankles and held it up for inspection. "Most people—people who are not like you and I—would have tried to barter rather than attempt an escape." His thick accent wrapped around each word, morphing it into something that Dotty's ears struggled to understand.

She used all her strength and pulled herself into an upright position. "We are not alike, you and I."

"That is not true," Sal said with a wag of his finger. "We both have la familia to protect. Your gang is yours, and the Blood Eagles are mine."

"You're a bunch of killers!"

Sal grabbed Dotty by the chin and held her with a bruising grip. "You came in the night and slaughtered the rest of us. And we are the killers? Don't forget who started this war."

"Lies!" she hissed. Dotty jerked her head back and out of his grasp. "I attacked your hideout. That much is true. But I only fought evil men, the filth of the west—men who deserved nothing less than the same torment they subjected others to."

"Is that what you tell yourself?" Sal chuckled. "And who gave you the right to judge them? I know your soul is just as stained with sin as theirs."

"So that is why you burned Black Lake to the ground? Vengeance?" Dotty shook her head. She was tired of outlaws and their need for revenge. Even her father behaved as though the world owed him something and the rest of civilized society had wronged him somehow. "Innocent people have lost everything! Mothers have lost their sons, and children are now without their parents because of your vile act of vengeance."

"And it is only just beginning," claimed her captor.

"Just kill me and get it over with."

"No, I do not think I will." Sal scratched at his jaw. His dark gaze stared into Dotty's eyes as if he really could see down to her soul. "I want you to suffer. I want you to watch as the world burns and know that it is because of you."

"No…" Dotty whispered. "I won't let you." Tears welled in her hazel eyes.

She thought of the story Steven had told her about how Budd heroically saved a child from a burning building. He had shown a selflessness and bravery that she lacked. Had she truly caused all the chaos?

Was Dotty the reason behind Salazar's cruelty? Questions rolled around in her mind until she feared they might drive her mad.

"And when you are surrounded by death and fire, I will kill Budd Mansfield," Salazar said with a smile.

"Salazar," snapped a man who hovered in the doorway. His bright eyes and dark hair marked him as Ripley Eagleson. Handsome and full of youthful energy, and yet there was a shadow behind his eyes that made Dotty uneasy.

"What is it?" asked Sal.

"Leave us," ordered Eagleson. "Go find Pete and have him count the loot."

Sal stood up and said something in Spanish that Dotty couldn't understand. He walked out of the small room, and Dotty glimpsed the rest of the small building.

It was some sort of hunting cabin nestled in the wilderness. The ceiling bowed, and the walls leaned to one side as if they struggled to hold up the weight of the roof.

There was no sound of voices or wagons outside. No sign they were still in Sacramento.

Still, she kept her wits about her and watched Ripley Eagleson like a hawk. The gang leader swaggered over to a decanter in the corner. Like the finely dressed man himself, the crystal seemed out of place in the cabin. He poured himself a glass and smiled at Dotty from over his shoulder. Though it was clear Ripley Eagleson was a handsome man, the smile left Dotty feeling soiled.

"Dorothy Valentine," Eagleson said as if he savored the name. "You have been a thorn in my hide since the day we met."

"I could say the same about you." Dotty wiped her tears on her shoulder, dampening the fabric of her torn and sullied dress. "It's been a long time since we last spoke."

"Too long." He took a sip of his drink and sighed. There was a look of contentment on his face that belied the nervous twitch in his leg. It bounced rapidly, shaking the floor beneath Dotty. "But we have Budd Mansfield to thank for reuniting us. After all, without his influence you would be back in Reno."

"I came to California on my own," she replied. "My plan was to put to rest the war between you and my father. Budd Mansfield has his own qualms against you."

"You came to do what, exactly? Kill me? Sway me?"

Dotty shook her head and said, "I know you will do the right thing. There's some goodness left inside you. The people you help, they speak highly of you even after learning of your deception."

***

Time seemed to slip through his fingers. Budd waited for Theodore Valentine for hours. Nightfall had crested over the distant hills, bringing a sense of foreboding. Buzzards still circled over the city. People gathered in the streets to mourn those killed in the raid. And still there was no sign of the gang leader.

At least, not until Budd had given up waiting. He turned to leave the empty lobby of the hotel and stopped in his tracks.

Theodore Valentine held a cigar between his fingers, staring down at the glowing ember as if in a trance. "You say my daughter was taken," he rumbled. "Who took her?"

Budd removed his hat and slowly approached Valentine. "Salazar Torez. I reckon this has something to do with Dotty's attack on the Blood Eagles a few years ago."

"Yes, that very well may be true," Valentine replied. The enigmatic man stabbed out the cigar's flame and tucked the stub in his pocket. "And I suppose you're still here because you intend to go after her."

"That's correct."

"My previous attempt to persuade you not to get involved ended in failure. I see no point in repeating that mistake," Valentine said. "You and I will go together, then. Just the two of us, Mr. Mansfield."

"But what if—"

Valentine held his hand up, cutting off Budd's rant. "I do not trust anyone else with my daughter's well-being. Either we go alone, or I have my associate keep you occupied while I go on my own."

He disliked the dark threat thinly veiled behind propriety. "I didn't come here to argue with you," Budd replied. "All I care about is finding Dotty and bringing her back alive."

"Then we have an agreement?"

With the city still recovering from the attack, Budd saw no reason to drag anyone else into the situation. He shook Valentine's hand and headed out to the stables, where Ivory waited in a stall. She perked up the second she sensed his presence. Budd embraced his horse, giving her a few loving pats on the side. He then saddled her up for the journey ahead. "You ready, girl?" Budd whispered.

Ivory tossed her mane and snickered.

Valentine entered the stables a moment later. His associate secured several saddlebags to a gray appaloosa. The gang leader said nothing as he prepared his horse.

It was clear to Budd that Dotty's disappearance weighed heavily on the man's shoulders. After all, she had come to Sacramento looking to clear the Valentine name.

"We'll sweep the valley and then head toward Yosemite," Budd said. "Rip likes to hide out near the forest. It gives him lots of cover in case of attacks."

"You seem to know a lot about how Ripley Eagleson thinks." Valentine gave Budd a probing look. "How do you know so much?"

"I've captured a few of his men. They've been forthcoming about how the gang operates."

"Forthcoming? That does not sound like the Blood Eagle Gang to me."

"Well, they were forthcoming after a few hours of persuasion," Budd replied. "I'll leave it at that. After all, Eagleson should have known he couldn't keep outlaws' quiet forever. Loyalty has limitations with criminals."

"Ripley Eagleson has loyalty to no one."

"He treats his gang like family."

Valentine shook his head. "He doesn't intend to pay them a penny," claimed the gang leader. "I have someone in my employment—a maid who keeps a close eye on Ripley's sister Beatrice. She reports Beatrice and her brother have been lying to the gang, that they send letters full of lies to the men saying the money is going to their families."

"But Eagleson keeps the money for himself?" Budd could hardly believe Ripley Eagleson was so devious to the men he called his brothers. The gang risked their lives each time they rode out of the Old Mill to provide for their families, and it was all for nothing.

He balked at the idea of such a betrayal. Though he had very few friends, Budd liked to think he was fair and just. He came to Sacramento with nothing but an idea, and he was grateful for the small bonds he had made.

"Ripley Eagleson cares for no one but himself." Valentine offered Budd a cigar as they left the stables. "But taking hostages isn't his way. Salazar will have a lot to answer for."

Budd wasn't sure about that. He knew Ripley Eagleson as a man capable of anything if he was desperate enough. But the last thing he wanted was for Dotty to get taken.

"If his aim truly is to end Pratt and Dempcy, he may have succeeded. Mr. Thayer will be bedridden for weeks, and who knows if the company can afford to keep operating under these conditions."

"Pratt and Dempcy will have a hard time earning back the trust of their clients. And you are hoping my daughter won't be harmed because he'll see this as a victory?"

"Yes," Budd answered honestly. "But I have faith in Dotty. She's gotten me out of more messes than I care to admit."

"Salazar took her because of me. Dorothy would never have attacked the Blood Eagles if I had done my job right as a leader and as a father," said Valentine. "And she came to Sacramento to make sure I wasn't a hunted man."

Budd led Valentine out of town. "I ain't gonna lie. Some of the blame falls on you. But Dorothy Valentine does as she pleases. Ain't no man in the world who could tell her what to do." He drew up close to a nearby tree and searched for tracks. The trail was too muddled. Each mile took them further into the wilderness. Valentine and Budd surveyed the canyon all the way to Pine's Bluff. They circled around and followed the river into Yosemite Valley. Days passed out on the trail.

Too much time had gone by, and Budd feared they may never catch a lead.

Chapter 12

Ripley Eagleson paced outside the rundown hunting shack on the edge of the valley. He tossed stones over the cliff behind the back of the building, listening to the echo of them bouncing off the rock face.

It was an empty sound that mirrored the way he felt inside. Dotty must have thought she could confuse him—that he would have broken at the first tug of his heartstrings. But she had been wrong. Very wrong.

Her ploy did not fool Rip. He saw her for what she was, saw beyond the angelic face she showed the world. In the depths of Dotty's soul, she was an outlaw.

Perhaps even more so than her father had ever been. Rip was forced into the life of banditry and lies, but Dotty had been born into it.

Under ordinary circumstances, Rip would have been furious Salazar had taken a hostage. Ripley Eagleson wasn't the sort of man who hurt women. But he supposed Dorothy Valentine wasn't just any woman.

In his mind, she was leverage. He had already destroyed Pratt & Dempcy, so all that remained of his plan was...

"Control," said Rip. "That's what I want now. I want control of the entire valley and all the settlements in the region. Do you know how I get that?"

Dotty glared up at him from where she kneeled on the floor. "Taking it from my father," she replied. "By getting rid of me and the rest of the gang."

"That's correct," Rip chuckled. He walked over to Dotty and pulled a knife from his belt. He cut the binds around her wrists. The look of pure shock on her face was almost comical. "You are my guest here. Not a prisoner... at least not yet. There's still a chance for you to earn your freedom. A simple business opportunity if you will."

"I could just run."

"You could," Rip said with a nod. He smacked Pete with the back of his hand, and the sleeping man woke with a start. "Leave us. Now."

Pete scampered from the room. The smell of stale sweat and cigarettes followed behind him like a fog. Rip curled his lip in disgust and took a seat on the couch where Pete had previously slept.

He smoothed out a wrinkle in his trousers as he awaited Dotty's answer. It wasn't as if he expected an eager response.

"What sort of business opportunity?" Dotty asked.

"You are a capable leader. You've shown your skill and earned the respect of your men. I want to offer you a place in my paradise." Rip allowed himself a smile. "You see, Sacramento belongs to me. I control the roads, which means I control everything. Give me your share of the Royal Heart Gang and I will make you a key figure in my city."

"You think Sheriff Dawson or Budd Mansfield will let that happen?" Dotty snorted.

Rip's heart stopped for a second. "Sheriff Dawson is dead. I shot him myself."

Dotty stood up and rubbed the raw flesh of her wrists. Her dress was torn and spattered with blood and dirt, but she held an air of sophistication. "He's very much alive. Saw him in the infirmary with my own eyes. Looked as though he were on the mend."

"I shot him in the chest. No one survives a wound like that."

"No, you shot him in the shoulder," Dotty corrected. "He must have turned as you were pulling the trigger. Either way, I assure you, Mr. Eagleson, he is very much alive."

"It's his word against mine. And I think the city will be abhor learning he did nothing to help them during the attack put in place by your father—"

"My father?" Dotty whirled around and pinned him with a seething glare. "So that's your plan? Blame the Royal Hearts for your crimes?"

"Your father has quite the reputation around these parts," Rip chuckled. "It won't be hard to convince the impressionable people of Sacramento that I was merely a victim in Theodore Valentine's schemes."

"You'll never get away with this!"

"My dear, I already have." Rip smiled and ran a hand through his hair. "People will remember who I was—they will remember their beloved Reginald Pearce and look at how I dug my hands in the dirt and built this city up. My influence, my money, will convince them."

"Money you stole from innocent people."

"No one is innocent," Rip said as he left the room. He walked over to Pete and ordered, "Bring her food and water when she needs it and keep watch over her. Make sure our guest doesn't leave until I say so."

Rip walked out onto the front porch to where Sal waited, with a cigarette between his lips. He stood beside Sal and ripped the cigarette from the outlaw's mouth.

"What have I always said about taking hostages?" Rip asked. "We cannot afford to leave a trail. Taking a hostage means we are open to negotiating with the law. Seeing as I have no intention of doing so, that would make this a waste of my damn time!"

"I thought—"

"You didn't think at all, and that's your problem. Budd Mansfield is probably out there right now, hunting us down. It's what he does best, according to the Pinkertons. And it's because of you I now have to clean up this mess."

"What do you want me to do, jefe?"

"Nothing." Rip stepped down from the porch and whistled for Storm. The loyal horse slowly trotted up to Rip and nudged his hand. "I want you to do absolutely nothing. Stay here and make sure nothing else goes wrong. I'll head to the Old Mill and see if Hector and the others made it back."

***

Budd set up camp as Ivory drank from the river. He hauled three saddle bags down from Valentine's horse and laid out the bedrolls. For a man who wore finely tailored suits, Valentine had packed an impressive load. It gave Budd a glimpse into the past. A glimpse of how Valentine had lived on the land as an outlaw.

Questions buzzed in Budd's mind. He wondered how life had been back when outlaws still laid claim over the west. The dawn of civilization was upon them, and there wasn't much room for gangs like the Royal Hearts or Blood Eagles anymore.

It seemed to Budd there wasn't a corner of the map the law hadn't touched. And a man like Valentine was sure to have some interesting things to say about the matter.

Back when Budd worked for the Pinkertons, he hadn't given outlaws the chance to tell their story. In his mind, bandits and outlaws were just faithless criminals.

But men like Evan Farris and Steven and Blake Wright had opened his eyes to the reality that things weren't so cut and dry. Even Dotty was wanted for one thing or another in half of the settlements in the region.

Budd turned toward Valentine just as the fire sparked to life. "What made you move your operation to Nevada?" he asked as he took a seat on his bedroll. "California is still mostly untouched. You could have moved further west."

"Unlike most gangs, our goal was never about claiming the west or revenge," Valentine answered. "It was about living under my own conditions. I had an ill wife and small daughter to provide for. We were starving while I was breaking my back in the mines, handing gold and iron over to men who refused to pay more than a few dollars a day."

Budd nodded along with Valentine's story. After all, it was identical to many of the people Budd knew in Sacramento. "So, you turned to banditry?" Budd asked.

"It was small things at first. Stealing food and a few trinkets here and there, but then I took claim over the mines I had worked for three tireless years. The other miners joined me, and we rose above our employers. The money was good at first, too." Valentine continued, "The men stayed loyal, and I kept their families fed. We moved on to robbing trains after that."

"That's how you became wanted in the territory? Robbing trains?"

Valentine took a swig from a silver flask before he answered. "Yep. Used the money to fund legitimate business in Nevada and settled the gang in Reno. With money coming in from the businesses, there was no need to rob trains anymore."

"How did Dotty become wanted?" Budd asked. He poked at the fire with a stick and stared into the flames as if they held all the answers. "She has quite the fighting spirit."

"My daughter was raised by a gang of outlaws, Mr. Mansfield," Valentine laughed. "I was lucky she learned any manners at all. Lord above knows she can out-drink most men and swear better than any sailor."

"So, it was inevitable."

Valentine shook his head and took another swig from his flask with a hiss. "I tried to keep her from following in my footsteps, but Dotty saw this world for what it was. Women ain't left with a lot of choices. And she refused to live her days as some rich man's property."

"I have a hard time seeing Dotty as any man's property," Budd snorted. "Rich or poor."

Valentine gave Budd an odd look. "Dotty means the world to me, Mr. Mansfield. But the two of you want different things in life."

Budd fell silent.

"If your intentions are to settle down and build a life in Sacramento," Valentine continued. "Then my daughter ain't the one for you. She'd rather die than see disappointment in your eyes every day. My Dotty ain't the wifely sort. She ain't gonna sit home and look after your house while you go off chasing outlaws."

"My intentions are to let her make her own decisions," Budd replied, though he'd be lying to himself if he said he wasn't upset.

Had he imagined a life with Dotty? Budd wasn't sure what he wanted. He had no expectations outside of capturing Ripley Eagleson. "And, with all due respect, I'd ask you to do the same. Dotty is her own woman, and she wouldn't like us discussing her future like we have any say in it."

"Very well," Valentine said. "What of the Blood Eagle Gang? Have you captured them yet?"

"We have Charles Wright and Hector Vasquez. Leroy Murphy goes to trial next week. We have until then to get the rest of them, or our case against Eagleson is meaningless," Budd replied. "We need all living members of the gang to speak against Ripley Eagleson, or he goes free."

"Any word from the marshal's office?" Valentine corked his flask and opened a tin of beans with his knife. "I heard

Dawson sent a letter after the telegraph operator was found."

"It's true. Dawson sent a letter, and so did I." Budd reached over and dug around in his satchel for a telegram. "He'll arrive any day now. Evan believes he'll want a full report on what's been happening. A lot of which is hard to prove without Eagleson behind bars."

"We'll get him."

"I hope so," Budd said. "In the beginning, I was doing this for Pratt and Dempcy. Now, I'm doing it for all Eagleson's victims and the people of Black Lake."

Chapter 13

The shack trembled with each gust of wind. Storm clouds swirled in the sky. Dotty stared out the window, searching for any chance of escape.

She needed a weapon. No, she needed a miracle. Dense clusters of trees surrounded the old hunting lodge, but beyond the trees was a steep cliff. There was one road that led away from the shack—a road closely watched by Salazar.

Dotty's skin crawled each time she thought of the outlaw and his wicked smile. Her gut told her Sal's thirst for revenge went beyond his loyalty to Ripley Eagleson. After all, Dotty had destroyed their old fort and cut down their numbers without mercy.

Part of her wondered if she deserved any sympathy. Was she no different from the gang she swore to destroy?

The door opened suddenly. Salazar stood in the entrance with a blade in his hand. Dotty wondered to herself how many of the stagecoach passengers had come face to face with such a vile-looking knife. It was long and wide, with a hook at the end. Someone had beautifully carved the handle from charred oak. Its sharp edge twinkled in the room's light.

"Looks like we might get some rain," Sal said. "Don't you worry, little bird. I will protect you from the storm."

"I need no protection." Dotty slammed her lips shut and cursed her sharp tongue. Last thing she needed was to anger her captor more. "What's the plan, huh? Bargain with my father for my safe return?"

Sal tsked. "There will be no bargaining," he said. "Money is not what I want."

"You want me dead."

"Sí."

"But you aren't in charge," Dotty said brazenly. "Ripley Eagleson wants me alive. Clearly, he has a plan. One I'm guessing he doesn't trust you with."

"He trusts me."

"My father trusted you once too," she snapped. "And you betrayed him by allying yourself with his enemy."

"Rip pays me better." Sal stalked toward her like a beast, inching closer with the grace of a true killer. "He sends the loot to my familia in Mexico. Your father never cared about my brothers and sisters or my uncle."

"Is that what he told you? That he cares about your family?" Dotty couldn't help but laugh as she watched Sal's brow furrow in confusion.

"Ripley Eagleson is a no-good snake in the grass. And you all will be dragged down with him when justice is finally served. Who will care for your family, then?"

Sal tapped Dotty's chest with his knife. "And what about you? What do you care deeply about?" He trailed the blade up toward her throat and pressed the tip into her skin. A single drop of blood trickled down and soaked into the fabric of her tattered dress. "Family? Your precious Royal Hearts...? Budd Mansfield?"

Dotty swallowed, and Sal's eyes sparkled with triumph. She watched as he sauntered out the door with that lecherous grin painted on his face. Once the door closed behind him, Dotty dropped to her knees on the floor.

She panted heavily, dragging mouthfuls of air into her lungs as she fought to control herself. Death had been so near. Sal could have killed her that very instant, but something stayed his hand.

Alone. Dotty was alone once again.

She scrambled across the floor and searched for a weapon beneath the bed, along the walls, and inside the bedside table. There were no knives, no hammers, or guns. It was clear to Dotty someone had cleared the hunting shack to prevent her escape.

Though Ripley Eagleson said she wasn't a prisoner, he hadn't said she was free to leave. Dotty was covered in dirt and grime and sweat.

She felt achy and miserable, but there was still fight left in her body. Her hands trembled as she reached for an oil lamp on the bedside table. It wasn't much, but it was all she had.

Dotty placed herself behind the door and waited.

Several minutes passed, and there was no sign of the outlaws. Doubt set in. In the back of her mind, Dotty knew there was only one way she could escape.

The trees would provide enough cover until she could get to the road, but there was a stretch of grass between the shack and the tree line where she would be in the open. It was a risk.

There was so much room for mistakes that it caused her heart to beat rapidly just at the prospect of following through with the plan. Dotty disliked feeling she had a target on her back.

She heard footfalls outside. Dotty readied herself. She gathered up her courage and lifted the lamp high. The young man, Pete, entered the room with a tray of food. She struck fast, smashing the oil lamp over his head. Glass cut through the skin on her fingers as it shattered, but Dotty grabbed his gun before he recovered.

"Against the wall," Dotty whispered harshly. "Quick! And no sudden moves."

Pete stumbled as he clutched a hand to his head.

"Is everything all right in there?" shouted Salazar from the other room.

"Tell him you dropped the tray," she ordered quietly.

"I-I dropped the tray, Sal. You know how clumsy I am." Pete placed his back against the wall. He held Dotty's gaze and stammered, "I ain't your enemy, miss. There are things goin' on you don't understand. I've been helpin' Budd Mansfield."

Dotty squinted her eyes suspiciously. "How so?"

"He let me go, didn't he?" Pete gestured to himself. "He captured me twice and let me go. I'm the one who told him about the attack on Leroy Murphy's transport to Reno."

"Help me get out of here," Dotty said. She placed all her cards on the table. It was a gamble, showing Pete the fear and desperation she felt inside. "Help me and no matter what happens to Ripley Eagleson, I will protect you."

"I don't know, ma'am..."

Dotty lowered the gun and held her hand out. "I promise. If you help me leave here alive, the Royal Hearts will protect you."

***

The Old Mill

Storm clouds obscured the sun as they rolled in. Gray fog spilled over the hills. The scent of rain stained the wind that rustled through the treetops.

A flash of lightning was followed by a rumble of thunder. Drops of water dotted the top of Ripley Eagleson's hat. A shiver raced down his spine as he approached the front gate.

Rip thought back to the time when he first learned about the Old Mill. He had heard the story of a city-slicker moving to the west to start a steel empire. But he had also heard the tales of how bandits had run the man off before construction had completed.

Which meant it was a prospective fortress hidden in the uncharted wilds of the California territory—a fortress ripe for the picking. Rip had laid claim to the Old Mill, and the Blood Eagles called it home for years before the likes of Budd Mansfield showed up.

Rip expected a warm greeting. Perhaps he even expected a feast to celebrate their victory. Pratt & Dempcy was unlikely ever to recover from the blow he dealt in the attack.

The raid had been just as successful as he planned. The only fault he saw was he hadn't put Sheriff Dawson down when he had the chance.

Even so, there was room for the lawman in Rip's brilliant new plan. It was one of his greatest yet, and one he had been looking forward to sharing with his gang. But his gang was nowhere in sight.

With Sal and Pete back at the shack, Rip had at least expected Hector and Charles within the Old Mill. They were gone. Vanished, as if they had never existed.

The Old Mill looked as abandoned as it had the day Rip had first discovered it.

George, one of Louis Bennett's men, ran up to Rip's horse with a letter clutched in his hand. It was a message from the city. Budd Mansfield and his men had captured Charles and Hector.

Rip crumpled the letter and tossed it onto the ground. He slid out of the saddle. His boots hit the dampened earth with a squelch. Mud splashed up onto his trousers but Rip hardly noticed. He pushed open the doors of the decrepit bones of the old steel mill and walked inside.

"How many are left?" Rip asked George.

"Seven, including us." George gestured to the room. "Everyone is dead or here in this room."

Injured outlaws and a handful of bandits littered the cavernous space. Many had been shot or maimed in during the attack on Sacramento. And for the first time since he founded the Blood Eagles, Ripley Eagleson felt truly alone.

Rip had lost everyone he had once called brother. Only Salazar and Pete remained of the gang. But one was a vicious killer, and the other was simply an incompetent fool.

"Do you want me to return to town?" asked George. "I can keep an eye on things until the law is not on our trail anymore."

Rip nodded. "Yes. You go back to Sacramento. Send a message if the marshal arrives while I'm gone. I want to be the first person who greets him."

George's brow furrowed with confusion. "You want to meet the marshal?"

"Why not? They'll be investigating stagecoach robberies that may or may not have been done by me. The good people of Sacramento still support me. After all, no one ever *saw* me committing any crimes." Rip brushed a hand over his suit and grimaced. He needed fresh clothes and a bath. "When all is said and done, it'll be the word of Budd Mansfield and corrupt lawmen against mine."

"What's the move, Eagleson?" asked a bandit who went by the name of Lucky Lewis.

"We focus on Mansfield." Rip looked into Lucky Lewis's eyes and saw fear, which disgusted him. "Do you have a problem with that, Mr. Lewis?"

Mansfield and his work for the Pinkertons was nearly as legendary as the Old Mill. It had taken more effort on Rip's part to convince his allies to help with the attack on Sacramento. Most of the outlaws in the region were too afraid of Mansfield and had refused to aid Rip.

It was a fear he had scoffed at in the beginning, but time had taught him Budd Mansfield was a formidable enemy. One he hadn't expected.

"No problem… it's just…" Lucky Lewis fidgeted with his belt as he rocked on his heels. "Budd Mansfield already caught so many of us. We're runnin' out of men."

Rip reached into his pocket and pulled out an ace of spades. He held it up for all to see. The eagle on the back of the card was a symbol of his strength, while the spade served as a warning to his enemies. A warning that Ripley Eagleson was not afraid to put someone six feet under.

"I'm giving you a choice. Take the card and deliver it to the sheriff for Mansfield," Rip said. "Or have it pinned to your thick head with my blade?"

"I'll deliver the message, sir."

"Good. It's time we sow doubt in the minds of the townsfolk," Rip replied. "Remind them Deputy Farris is a wanted man in the region and that Budd Mansfield is still an outsider."

He handed the card to Lucky Lewis and returned to Storm. The dark stallion waited obediently, despite the rain. Rip climbed back into the saddle and took the path away from the Old Mill. He headed toward Timber, where he intended to begin the next part of his plan.

Chapter 14

Budd was soaked through. Steam curled from his lips with each breath as he shivered. He crouched in the overgrown underbrush near the edge of an old path and picked up a familiar pistol.

Budd held the weapon up toward the lantern in his hand to inspect it further. There was no doubt in his mind the weapon belonged to Dotty. She had carved the Royal Heart Gang's insignia on the wooden handle.

Finally, after days of searching the forest, they had found a lead. One Budd hoped would lead them right to where Dotty was held hostage. Just the thought of her in the hands of vicious outlaws made Budd's stomach clench painfully.

He stood up from the dampened earth and made his way back toward Theodore Valentine. The wind and rain hadn't let up for hours. Drops of water obscured his vision, but he found the camp without much of a problem.

"Look here," he said as he approached. Budd showed the gun to Valentine. "Dotty can't be far. They tossed her weapons, or she dropped them. At least now we know we are headed in the right direction."

"The storm should pass soon. We can look in the morning," Valentine suggested.

Budd shook his head. "I want to search the area some more. Might be lucky enough to find some tracks before they're washed away."

He handed the gun to Valentine and turned back toward the area he had found the gun. His boots sank into the mud as he trekked through the underbrush once more. His lantern flickered wildly each time the wind blew. But there in the barely lit forest he found a set of fresh tracks.

Budd knew in his gut those tracks were the miracle he had been waiting for. He headed right back toward the camp and reported his finding to Valentine. The man was just as eager as Budd to find Dotty. So much so they packed up camp before the storm passed.

They moved alongside the tracks. Ivory slipped on the mud and nearly sent Budd flying out of the saddle. The rain stopped, but the chill of the night air lingered long after.

Flashes of lightning still streaked across the sky, but Budd believed the worst was behind them. The storm had passed, and the path ahead was clear.

Far off in the distance, a light flickered. Voices carried through the forest, reverberating off the trees. Budd recognized the voice of Pete Jones and cursed.

Pete was a spineless coward and a double-crossing snake most days. But there was a part of Budd that felt bad for Pete. The young man had been roped into Ripley Eagleson's mess once again. There was nothing else Budd could have done to help Pete.

Budd turned to where he had left Valentine and saw he had abandoned his horse. With a slew of foul words spilling from his lips, Budd hitched Ivory to a nearby tree and tracked Valentine down. He found his travel companion near a clearing in front of a rundown shack. It was some sort of hunting shelter that had been abandoned at some point before Ripley Eagleson's gang moved in. Valentine approached the shack as if he were fearless.

"Salazar Torez!" shouted Valentine. "You got my daughter in there, and I intend to leave here with her in hand."

A gunshot erupted from the shack.

Valentine stumbled back as a bullet hit him in the chest. Budd dashed over and knocked Valentine out of the way before the second shot was fired. He then dragged the older man behind a large rock and pressed a bandana to the wound. "Hold still," Budd hissed as he applied pressure. "He got you on the right side. Looks bad."

"Don't worry about me. Get my daughter home."

"She's coming back to Sacramento with us no matter what it takes," he replied. "What were you thinking? We could have been walking into a trap."

"Had… to… let her know. Let her know someone came for her, th-that she wasn't alone." Valentine took the scrap of cloth from Budd's hand and held it against his own chest. "Go get my daughter. I'll hold them off."

Budd ducked as another shot rang through the forest. He leaped from behind his cover and fired his gun at the shack. In the chaos, Budd reached the front door.

He kicked it open, startling the man near the window. Salazar whipped around and aimed his gun at Budd, but Budd was too quick. He knocked the gun out of Salazar's hand. The outlaw roared and tackled Budd. They crashed through a table and landed on the floor in a pile of rubble.

A punch landed against Budd's jaw, followed by an explosion of pain. Salazar reared his arm back for another blow. Budd grabbed the outlaw by the shirt and rolled on top of him before the punch landed.

They grappled wildly, taking turns landing hits that made Budd dizzy. He shook his head and felt a trickle of blood ooze from his nose.

"I should have killed you a long time ago," said Salazar. He tore out of Budd's grasp and pulled a blade from his boot. The outlaw wielded the blade with expert precision. Budd ducked and dodged each slash through the air.

At the last second, Salazar arched the blade upward and caught Budd across the torso. The sharp edge cut straight through his shirt and down to the skin. A long, scarlet stain appeared.

"You don't know how many times I've heard outlaws say that," Budd retorted. "Funny thing is they're always right. You only get one chance to kill me. After that, you best hope I ain't on your trail, or else you'll end up in a cell or in a grave."

***

Dotty locked eyes with Pete as a commotion came from the other room. Had she heard her father's voice? She desperately hoped he hadn't come out of hiding to find her.

Dotty gripped the gun tightly and moved back toward the door. She listened carefully. Voices, muffled by the door, met her ears.

"Give yourself up, Torez," said Budd Mansfield. Dotty's heart leaped at the sound of his deep growl.

"You will have to kill me!"

Dotty pushed open the door with her shoulder and fired at Salazar. The outlaw jumped back with a shout and charged toward Dotty. Pete got between them, taking the force of the charge against his side, colliding with the wall.

Budd crawled to his feet and cocked the hammer on his pistol. "Hands up," he snarled. "I won't tell you twice."

Dotty stepped around Pete and Salazar. She made her way to Budd's side as Salazar finally surrendered. Her eyes watched the outlaw carefully.

Part of Dotty knew her captor was capable of deception far greater than Budd might expect. So, she stayed close and kept her senses sharp.

Budd yanked Salazar by the arm and forced him to his knees. He took a length of rope from his belt and hogtied the outlaw. Salazar shouted in Spanish, cursing the three of them in ways they couldn't understand.

But the seething rage in his voice was evident. Those dark eyes glared into Pete.

Dotty felt a twinge of sympathy for the young bandit. After all, he had saved her from Salazar's violence. She owed him for that. Pete could have sided with his friend and taken on Budd without a hitch.

Instead, Pete had risked Salazar's wrath and helped Budd. "Thank you, Mr. Jones." Dotty reached out to shake his hand, but Budd Mansfield clapped him in irons before she got the chance.

They led the captured outlaws toward the horses outside. Dotty's father leaned against his horse. There was a bloody wound in his chest. Dotty panicked.

She rushed over and tore open her father's vest. Her fingers prodded around the wound, and she hissed through tightly clenched teeth. The wound was deep, and his face was ashen.

"Pa!" Dotty shouted. "You were supposed to disappear. It was for your own safety."

"My safety means nothing if you are in danger."

Dotty shook her head. "I can take care of myself. You know that," she argued. "It was foolish to come here." She raced back into the shack.

She searched for bandages, medicine, thread... anything that might help, only to come up empty. Out of options, Dotty wandered into the room where she had been held. She tore the linens on the bed into strips of fabric for makeshift bandages. She hurried back to her father and used them to keep the wound covered. Her father groaned and complained, but he was too weak to put up a real fight.

"Can you help me?" Dotty asked as she struggled to get her father onto his horse. Budd helped Dotty get her father into the saddle before he climbed onto Ivory's back.

She then rode back to Sacramento with the others on Salazar's ornery horse.

The angry beast almost bucked her out of the saddle four or five times along the way. But Dotty held on tight and kept a close watch on her father. He grew paler by the second. The infirmary was just up ahead.

Dotty helped her father down from his horse and all but dragged him into the doctor's office. A nurse gasped at the sight of them. Suddenly, Dotty was forced to release her father into the doctor's care.

She stood at the center of the room, feeling rather lost, as he was placed upon a small cot in the corner. The curtain closed, blocking her view. Horrible screams came from her father until an eerie silence fell over the infirmary.

Budd pulled Dotty outside. "You should get cleaned up and eat something."

"I'll eat when I know what is happening with my father."

"You ain't doing him any favors by starving yourself," Budd stated firmly. "Knowing you're all right will help him heal. Trust me."

Dotty felt her head bob up and down, but she felt as though someone else was in control of her body. She barely noticed the walk back to Budd Mansfield's home or the bath he prepared for her. Dotty only knew her father was suffering, and she was helpless to do anything about it.

The sound of the door closing snapped her out of her trance. It took a moment for her to realize she was in her bedchamber, standing just inches away from a steaming washtub.

The tattered remnants of her dress floated to the floor.

A pale foot dipped into the water, and a sigh of relief escaped her lips. Dotty slid deeper into the tub until she was submerged to her neck. She let the scalding water soothe her aching muscles.

In the quiet of dawn, Dotty allowed herself to cry. She cried for the people who had lost so much. She cried for Budd Mansfield and her father. And Dotty cried for herself. She cried until the water grew cold and her fingers wrinkled.

There was a new dress and slippers waiting for her when she stepped out of the tub. Dotty chewed her bottom lip thoughtfully. Budd Mansfield had gone out of his way to help her.

She owed him more than she cared to admit. "Budd," Dotty called when she left her bedchamber. "Thank you. I don't know how I'll repay you for the kindness."

He appeared in the corridor, freshly shaven and dressed. Budd wore a cotton work shirt, leather suspenders, and a pair of trousers. His unruly hair had been combed back from his face, and the old boots she had grown accustomed to had been replaced by a pair of ordinary shoes.

It was odd for Dotty to see him looking as though he hadn't just come home from a long journey on the road.

"No reason to thank me, Dotty," he said. "I'll help you in any way you need."

Chapter 15

The saloon was in shambles. Glass peppered the floor, tables were on end, and sticky, congealed puddles of mysterious liquid covered the bar. Bullet holes riddled the walls, and the swinging door at the entrance had only one panel.

Budd shook his head at the sight of all the wreckage. He stepped over a broken chair and made his way over to where his men sat.

Blake, Steven, and Evan passed a bottle of whiskey between them. They looked up as he approached and lifted their glasses in a silent salute.

Evan scooted a chair over to Budd and took the bottle from Blake's hand. He poured Budd a drink, but Budd declined. "Not in a drinking mood, I see," Evan said. "How's Dotty?"

"She's been better," answered Budd. "Valentine was shot in cold blood. The doctor ain't too sure if he'll make it. I'll keep him in my prayers, but there's only so much the doc can do. Medicine is in short supply after the attack."

Evan whistled as he ran a hand through his hair. "Valentine ain't a good man, but from what I heard, he's a noble father. I hope he pulls through, for Dotty's sake."

Budd sat down with a huff and stretched out his long legs beneath the table. He looked around at the empty saloon once again and thought back to the first time he stepped foot inside the door.

Though he hadn't been in Sacramento for long, Budd had made many lasting memories. Both good and bad. He just hoped this wasn't the end for Sacramento.

Ripley Eagleson didn't deserve the satisfaction.

"What's the plan movin' forward?" asked Blake Wright. "We've got the whole gang, except Eagleson. Is it enough to convince the marshal?"

Budd shook his head. "Not if they aren't willing to come clean. It'll just be a waste of time without Eagleson. With him out, they'll hang on to hope he'll break them free."

He scrubbed a hand over his face and sighed, "We have to find the Old Mill. What we need is there. I just know it. I feel it in my gut."

Blake took a swig from his glass. "I searched everywhere," he replied. "Whatever path Leroy Murphy was talkin' about... I ain't found it yet."

"It's no secret we've all been distracted lately. We'll find it. Don't worry," Evan said. "Pete and the others will talk. Eventually they'll have to."

"I'm not so sure," Steven chimed. "Budd's right. We need to get evidence on Eagleson. That's the only way to put an end to this the right way."

There was one big piece of the puzzle missing: Beatrice Pepper. "Steven, I need you to go to Reno. See if you can find where Eagleson's sister is hiding with all the loot," Budd said. "Blake and I will question the gang about the whereabouts of the Old Mill. Evan, you stay by Sheriff Dawson's side. Make sure there're no more attempts on his life. Last thing we need is to lose more men to Ripley Eagleson."

The men nodded along with his every word.

"We need to have this all figured out before the marshal arrives, or else the gang will walk free," he continued. "The fate of this city is resting on our shoulders. Let's not make any more mistakes."

They parted ways. Steven headed for the stables, while the others walked toward the sheriff's office. Budd took the lead. He opened the door and scowled at the cell packed to the brim with outlaws.

Salazar Torez, Charles Wright, and Hector Vasquez sat in opposite corners. None of the men spoke to one another as Budd leaned against the bars. He kept his tone sharp and to the point. "The Old Mill. Where is it?" he asked. "Give me the location, and I might just be willing to make you a deal when the marshal gets to town."

Salazar spat on the floor near Budd's boots. "We will tell you nothing."

Budd walked past Salazar and leaned closer to Hector. "What about you, huh? Are you willing to talk, or do I have to get creative with how I ask?"

"Where is Pete?"

"Dead," lied Budd easily. "Pete Jones hit his head hard when he fought off Salazar. Poor kid had a weak constitution. I'm surprised he made it to town long enough for the doctor to see him."

Budd and Dotty had both agreed it was best to send Pete away for his own safety. The kid had done right by them, and it was the least they could do to keep Ripley Eagleson from coming after him.

"Good riddance!" shouted Charles from the back wall. "Serves him right for turnin' his back on this gang! Should have done away with him a long time ago."

Budd was tired of talking in circles. He snatched the key ring from a hook on the wall and opened the cell. Blake grabbed onto Budd's arm, trying in vain to pull him back.

Budd was unstoppable. His fist crashed into the side of Charles's head. The outlaws jumped in. Blake held Salazar back while Budd took on Charles and Hector. Punches flew.

Salazar hit the ground. Blake climbed on top of the outlaw and held him down. "Budd! It ain't worth it! Come on. Pull yourself together!"

Budd took an elbow to the ribs and nearly toppled over. He kicked Hector square in the chest and sent him reeling backward. Charles was in his grasp. "Tell me where the Old Mill is!" he bellowed with rage. Before he could land another hit, deputies pulled him out of the cell.

In his mind, Budd was suddenly back in the burning house with a young child clutched to his chest. Anger and sadness warred within him.

A dark swarm of raw emotions overwhelmed Budd until they nearly lost him to the shadows. It was Dotty who pulled him back from the brink. Her smile filled his vision until he knew nothing else.

***

The morning sun warmed the carriage as it pulled to a stop near the stables.

Rip paid the driver and climbed out of the carriage with a cigar between his teeth. After a week in Timber, Rip was glad to be back in Sacramento. News of Pete Jones and Theodore Valentine's demise had come as a shock. One that was more of a pleasant surprise than he thought it would be.

Pete had always held a special place in Rip's heart. He had seen the young man as a little brother that was constantly getting into trouble.

Still, there was work that needed doing before the day was done.

Rip walked along the sidewalk. His shoes tapped rhythmically against the wooden planks that lined the road. Folks turned and looked in his direction as he passed. Many of the faces were familiar, but some weren't.

He reckoned they must have been from Black Lake. Though what they had done to the small town was a tragedy, there wasn't a drop of regret inside of Ripley Eagleson's cold, black heart. In fact, he prided himself on his ability to do what they needed despite the consequences.

For Sacramento to prosper beneath his rule, there were sacrifices that needed to be made. If he was the only one willing to make them, so be it. He loved the city and all its flaws.

He loved the tireless hours of the daily grind and the quiet nights filled with liquor and women. Sacramento was a living, breathing thing to Rip. Something that needed to be nurtured, so it might grow into something spectacular.

He admired it in all its glory as he made his way down to the mayor's office. Rip was careful as he opened the door and stepped inside the rundown building.

The woman behind the desk looked exhausted. Dark circles rested beneath her eyes, and there was tension at the corner of her mouth as she smiled up at him. "Hello. How can I help you, sir?"

"I'm here to see Mayor Thomas," Rip replied politely.

"We are in the middle of rebuilding. Do you have an appointment?"

Rip pinched the bridge of his nose in irritation. "Tell him Mr. Eagleson would like to speak with him immediately. It is a matter of utmost urgency."

"Very well." The young woman shuffled off down the corridor. The sound of her heels clicked on the hardwood floors. She opened the door at the far end of the hall and disappeared. Hushed whispers floated down the hall a second before the door opened again. "He will see you now."

Rip nodded his thanks and followed the woman into the mayor's office.

"I don't know if it is bravery or stupidity that brings you here, but… it's good to see you, Eagleson," said Mayor Thomas. "I once thought of us as friends. Perhaps when you were going by the name of Reginald Pearce, we were."

"I come here out of desperation," replied Rip. He sat down in the chair across from the mayor's desk. "Budd Mansfield has tainted my reputation for long enough."

Mayor Thomas paced behind his desk for a moment. "Mansfield? What does he have to do with anything?"

"Don't you see?" asked Rip with tears in his eyes. "Mansfield used my name to cover up his crimes. And that Sheriff Dawson is behind it too. They slandered my name while stealing thousands of dollars from Pratt and Dempcy! They're thieves and killers. The lot of them."

Mayor Thomas leaned over the desk. He placed his hands flat on the surface and hung his head. "Why you, huh? Why not anyone else?"

"Because I was a beacon of hope for this town," Rip claimed. "I had to hide—had to change my name so Budd Mansfield wouldn't kill me. You've seen it yourself. He's infiltrated this city with outlaws. Dorothy Valentine, Evan Farris, and those Wright boys. And Sheriff Dawson let them in!"

"You mean Mansfield is behind it all?" Mayor Thomas scratched at his head in confusion. "Mr. Thayer speaks so highly of him."

"Despite my own complicated past with Howard, I wish him the best in his recovery. But he cannot speak highly of anyone at the moment." Rip pressed a hand to his chest in a sign of sincerity. "You said we were friends, and I truly wish to believe that. I took a risk coming to see you today. Help me. Please."

"I don't know..."

"Think about it, my friend," said Rip. "We've always had trouble with gangs. A few robberies here and there. But all this chaos started not long after he arrived."

Rip reached into his pocket and pulled out a letter that the Pinkertons had written. He set it on the desk in front of the mayor and waited.

Mayor Thomas unfolded the letter. His eyes darted across the page. "They released Mansfield from his contract after he attacked one detective. They described him as unstable and highly unpredictable," said the mayor. "And the Pinkertons are on their way here to arrest Budd Mansfield."

"There's a man here in town I think you should talk to about this. He knows Mansfield better than anyone," he said. "Douglas Buchanan is his name. He'll tell you just how untrustworthy Budd Mansfield really is."

"I know Buchanan and his wife, Rose. They're good people. I recall them mentioning Douglas's work with the Pinkertons," replied Mayor Thomas. "I'll look into this. I promise. But in the meantime, keep your head down and find someplace to stay."

Chapter 16

Outskirts of Sacramento, California
November 1880

Crickets chirped loudly as nightfall crested over the hills in the distance. Dark clouds chased away the sun. Dotty watched as Pete shoveled another pile of dirt onto the oak coffin at the bottom of a large hole in the ground.

She dabbed away the tears that rolled down her cheeks and whispered a prayer for her father. Her fingers turned white as she gripped the lantern tighter. The amber light cast ghostly shadows on Pete's face.

It wasn't long before the hole was filled and Pete hobbled over to her. Dotty brushed the dirt from his clothes and sighed. So much had changed in the days that followed her father's death.

She had inherited her father's gang in Reno, gained a significant amount of money, and became the sole owner of the Valentine estate. But she would have traded everything just to have him back.

"I'm sorry about your father, ma'am."

"Thank you, Pete."

The two of them stood beside the freshly dug grave with their heads bowed.

"What will happen to me when we get to Reno?" he asked nervously. "I'm done with crime. I promise… it's just that I don't really have many skills doin' other things."

"You'll work for me at the estate," she answered. "There will be plenty of work, and I intend to pay fair wages. I understand you have two sisters to care for."

"Eva and Julianna. They're countin' on me."

"Your sisters are welcome to come to the estate."

A bright smile came over his face. Pete jumped for joy and threw his arms around Dotty in a big bear hug. He blushed from head to toe when he pulled away. "Thank you."

"Come," she said to Pete. "Let us say our goodbyes and head to Nevada."

"Yes, ma'am."

The young man obediently followed Dotty back to the edge of town. She led him into the city and to Budd Mansfield's home. She opened the door just after midnight and greeted Budd with a gentle smile. "Good evening. I hope you don't mind us visiting…"

"You two should be on a train headed east by now," grumbled Budd. "I risked a lot by telling everyone Pete was dead. If the gang finds out he's alive, they won't hesitate to come after him."

Dotty understood his caution, even if she resented it. She respected Budd, but she wished he would let his guard down a bit. He knew her feelings toward him, yet he hadn't acted upon them.

Sure, she supposed courtship had been the furthest thing from his mind, but it hadn't seemed impossible, even under the circumstances. "I couldn't leave without saying goodbye," Dotty said softly. "And I believe our friend Mr. Jones here has something he'd like to share with you."

Pete nodded enthusiastically and pulled a tattered old map from his pocket. He handed it off to Budd with a smile, and Dotty felt proud of the young man. "It's a map of the Old Mill," said Pete. "And all the hidden pathways the boss used to take."

Budd looked at the map in awe. "This... this could change everything. We could finally find where Eagleson's been hiding the stolen goods."

"You'll have to move quickly," replied Pete. "Every month he sends a wagon to Reno for his sister Beatrice to look after. She then sends the money to our families... or at least that's what we used to think."

Budd and Dotty locked eyes for a moment. They knew the truth about Ripley Eagleson. It just about broke Dotty's heart to think anyone could have been so cruel.

There was very little in the world that she deemed more important than family. Whether it was by blood or by bond, Ripley Eagleson should have protected his family.

"We'll look into it immediately," Budd stated.

She pulled Budd aside and took his hand in hers. "I won't be doing anything about it," Dotty said. "With my father's death... someone must look after the estate. It's my responsibility. I know I promised to see this through, but—"

"Don't worry about it," Budd interrupted. "We can't predict what will happen next. It would be best if you were safe in Reno until this is all over. I know it would put my mind at ease. I don't want to think about what it would do to me if something happened to you."

Dotty's heart leaped. She swallowed past the lump in her throat and bit back a smile. It was no surprise to her that Budd cared, but the sincerity in his eyes had caught her off guard. There was more in his gaze than she suspected he was aware.

In fact, if not for the stubborn set of his shoulders, Dotty would bet he was in love with her. She pushed up onto the tips of her toes and pressed a kiss to his cheek.

"Promise me you'll reach out if anything changes," she whispered. "Just send word, and I'll ride to Sacramento whenever you need me."

Budd looked as though he wanted to argue. Instead, he wrapped his arms around her. The gentleness of his touch took her breath away. "I promise," he said. "There's no one else I would trust at my back. Evan and the others... It's just different with them. You've saved me, Dotty. In more ways than I think you know."

She finally allowed herself a small smile. The smell of his soap lingered in her nose long after he released her from his hold. It was like she had wanted to keep a part of him with her on her travels. "Look how far you've come. When I arrived, you were in love with Rose Buchanan. Now you're all but proposing to me."

Budd snorted and shook his head. He stepped back, glancing up and down at her as though committing her image to memory. "Always with the exaggerations, Miss Valentine."

"What's life without a little embellishment, Mr. Mansfield?" she chuckled. Dotty held her hand out and asked, "Shall we part as friends?"

***

Timber, California

The stagecoach came into view just as the sun had risen. Rip and his riders waited near Timber with their guns drawn and their masks pulled high on the bridge of their noses.

Though he had hoped his gang would have been free for one last stagecoach, Rip was more than ready to work with the outlaws his allies had sent him. Each one of the men by his side played by different rules than his gang. They descended upon the stagecoach like a pack of hungry wolves.

Screams broke through the quiet of the morning.

Rip spurred Storm on, urging the large stallion to pull up beside the coach. He locked eyes with the driver and gestured for the man to stop. But Budd Mansfield and his meddling had instilled just enough courage in the driver that he foolishly disobeyed. Rip fired his gun at the man's feet.

The driver yelped and jumped off the bench, causing the stagecoach to crash into a cluster of nearby boulders. The men stopped alongside the stagecoach. They rounded up the driver and the guard, presenting them to Rip like some sort of offering. "Get the passengers too!" he ordered. "On their knees! Now!"

They pulled a wealthy man and his two sons from the stagecoach. The sons were clothed in the latest and most expensive of men's garb. Just by the look of their fobs, watches, and cufflinks, he knew they were well off.

They were the sort of folks Rip enjoyed robbing. The kind who had more money than they could ever spend in one lifetime. And it was time they spread the wealth a bit.

"Budd Mansfield," he drawled. "Repeat that name until the law arrives."

"W-what?" stammered the older gentleman.

Rip pressed his gun to the man's head. "Budd Mansfield. Say it."

"Budd Mansfield."

"Again," he sneered.

"Budd Mansfield."

"Why am I doin' this?" Rip asked as the man repeated the name several more times. Round and round, the name went. He lowered his gun. "Who robbed you today?"

"B-Budd Mansfield."

"Very good." Rip smiled behind his mask. He listened to the name of his enemy as it fell from the lips of the gentleman. Each time the name was spoken, it brought him great joy, for it served as a reminder of how close he was to the second act of his plan.

Pratt & Dempcy was no more. There was nothing left for him to exact revenge upon. Therefore, he had set his sights upon the city. Sacramento was his and his alone.

The stagecoach creaked as his men tore it apart in search of valuables. He had promised them loot, and loot was what they got. The wealthy man and his sons were prospectors. There were nuggets of gold tucked away inside their bags.

Even a crate of iron ore was worth more than the watches and fobs, but those were taken as well.

Once the men were stripped of their valuables, the gang mounted up for the ride back into town. They separated and marked up the paths around the stagecoach with indiscernible tracks to avoid being followed.

"Let's get a drink," Rip grumbled to his men. "We deserve one after all we've accomplished. Pratt and Dempcy fell beneath our might, and we showed Sacramento who was really in power. The Blood Eagle Gang remains strong, and it's because of all of you."

Rip retreated to the hotel and changed into his clothes. He stashed away his gear in a sack hidden beneath the floorboards. The owner gave him a knowing look as he walked down to the lobby.

Rip paid the usual fee and extra for the man's discretion. There weren't many places an outlaw could call home, but Timber had proven to be an irreplaceable haven for men like him. Timber embraced criminals with open arms.

They regrouped at the saloon, where they raised their glasses in celebration. A chorus of cheers sounded through the hall. Rip sat at the head of the table with a soiled dove in his lap and a drink in his hand.

He watched as the men chatted among each other, sharing stories of their greatest conquests. It was he who had brought them together—men who would have been enemies under different circumstances. And it was their shared hatred of the law that put that spark of defiance in their gazes.

"To a job well done," Rip said as he lifted his glass once more.

"Here, here!"

"Way to go, boss!"

"Couldn't have done it without you, boss!"

"To Rip," said Lucky Lewis.

Rip grinned from ear to ear as he set the girl aside. He pulled Lucky Lewis over to the card table and gestured for the other men to deal them into the game. Cards slid across the green fabric and landed right in front of Rip's drink. He peered down at his hand, and his smile grew tenfold.

"I wanted to thank you, Lucky," Rip slurred, eyes blurry from one too many drinks. "And I wanted to ask if you would like to help me with something."

"Anything for you, Rip," replied Lucky Lewis. The outlaw put his arm around Rip's shoulder and nodded.

Rip kept his voice low and leaned toward Lucky Lewis. "I'm going to bust my men out of that jailhouse and pin it on Budd Mansfield. I'll need your help and a few more fellers to get it done."

"Mansfield has gotten in the way one too many times."

"My thoughts exactly," Rip snorted. "He'll no doubt take it upon himself to investigate our job from this morning. If he comes poking around, you know what to do. Otherwise, keep your heads down, and I'll come find you when it's time to bust my men out."

Lucky Lewis took a swig of his beer and slammed the glass onto the floor. "You got it, boss. I'll stick around here when y'all go back to the Old Mill."

Rip turned his cards over and said, "Blackjack." The dealer pushed the winnings toward Rip before he dealt another hand. It seemed luck was on his side.

Chapter 17

Sacramento, California

Bang! Bang! Bang!

"Open up!"

The sound of someone pounding on his door woke Budd. He tossed his legs over the side of the bed and stood up with a grunt. Bare feet shuffled across the floor, down the stairs, and toward the front door.

Remnants of a fire still crackled in the hearth as Budd glanced around his home. Dotty was gone. It was what he expected, but painful. "Wait a minute!" he shouted when the knocks became impatient.

The door opened.

Budd winced as the sun scorched his eyes. He lifted an arm to shield his vision and took in the sight of Sheriff Dawson in shackles. The lawman's jaw was clenched so hard that Budd feared he might crack his teeth. But the marshal's badge twinkled in the sunlight, distracting Budd from his sleepy train of thought. "What can I do for you?"

"Mr. Budd Mansfield," said the marshal. "I'll ask you to come with us, please."

"What for?"

"My name is Eddison Greene," replied the marshal, as if he hadn't heard Budd's question. "And with the authority of the U.S. Marshal's office, I have a warrant here for your immediate arrest."

Budd's eyes shot open. "There must be a mistake. I have done nothing wrong, and neither has the sheriff."

"Come outside. Slowly and with your hands where I can see them."

Budd stood still. He shook his head and nearly stumbled. The shock of the marshal's words was too much. Had he done something? Had Sheriff Dawson? he wondered to himself. "Please… just tell me what I did."

Marshal Greene waved his hand, and deputies stepped forward with cuffs. They pushed Budd up against the wall and secured his hands. Budd's mind struggled to keep up as they forced him out of his home and onto the streets. It was then he noticed Evan, Blake, and Steven beside Sheriff Dawson.

"Tell me what I'm being arrested for," Budd snapped. "I ain't done nothing wrong! You've got the wrong man!"

"Witnesses have come forward, Mr. Mansfield," Marshal Greene said finally. "Witnesses who saw six bandits attack Pratt and Dempcy stagecoaches. Imagine how surprised I was when I received word from Mayor Thomas. He told me you, Sheriff Dawson, Evan Farris, Blake Wright, Steven Wright, and the elusive Miss Dorothy Valentine were all identified by Ripley Eagleson as the ones responsible for the attacks."

"Ripley Eagleson is the one responsible!"

Marshal Greene turned toward Budd and shook his head. "There's no talking your way out of this one. Mr. Buchanan has already spoken about your character. Not to mention the traumatized man who was rescued this morning who wouldn't stop muttering your name! But it was none of them that secured your fate, Mr. Mansfield. It was the written statement of Howard Thayer that—"

"Ripley Eagleson attacked Mr. Thayer when the town was nearly taken over by Eagleson's gang!" Budd argued.

"Howard remembers nothing of an attack. He only recalls barely being conscious and hearing you and Blake Wright bursting into his office." Marshal Greene yanked Budd over by his shackles and glared right into his eyes. "He also filed a document stating you had withheld knowledge of attacks from the company and worked directly with known outlaws. Face it, your time here is over."

Budd clenched his hands into fists. "You're being played like a fiddle, Greene."

"No, this city was being played by you in the beginning, but not anymore," replied Marshal Greene. "I'm here to set things right. And until that happens, you and your accomplices will remain behind bars."

Ripley Eagleson had won.

Budd lowered his head and avoided the gazes of his men. Though he wanted nothing more than to reassure them, there was nothing he could say to convince the marshal.

There was part of Budd that saw how the marshal and Mayor Thomas had drawn their conclusion. No longer could he deny the similarities between Ripley Eagleson and himself. Similarities that were both physical and intellectual.

With a mask on, anyone could mistake them. And hadn't Budd noticed the bandit leader's drawl when he spoke? One that was more like his own than Ripley Eagleson's. In that moment, Budd almost convinced himself he was guilty. He needed to talk to the witnesses and find out what had happened, but it was impossible from behind bars.

Budd thought of running. He thought of fighting. He even thought of lying to spare them from facing the gallows. But along with the others, he was led to the jailhouse and locked away like some sort of common thief.

The only solace he found was in knowing Dotty had gotten out of the city before the marshal arrived. She was safe and with her gang, and that eased part of his worries. "I'm sorry," Budd huffed as the cell closed behind him. "I'm sorry I dragged all of you into this. I should have been more careful."

"Shut up," said Evan. "We knew the risks."

Blake nodded and added, "Not like this is my first time in cuffs, either."

"But we're innocent," Budd sighed. "We risked our lives defending this city."

Sheriff Dawson sat on the cot beside Blake. He said, "I'm sure Ripley Eagleson has told them that too. Lord knows he was an upstanding citizen when he was Reginald Pearce. Compared to him, you're all little more than strangers to the people of this city. I haven't even been here as long as Eagleson has been. He has their trust."

"And I broke Mr. Thayer's trust when I allowed that gang to steal from the stagecoaches," said Budd. "I knew better. I should have just let him put a bullet in my head at that moment and saved us all the trouble of being locked up in here." He paced back and forth in front of the cell door.

Across the way was Ripley Eagleson's gang. Salazar had a smile on his face as he watched Budd with a predatory gaze.

"Hola, señor," Salazar chuckled. "How does it feel on the other side of the bars?"

Epilogue

Sacramento, California
December 1880

Something was wrong.

Budd felt a stirring in his gut. He sat up. Sweat beaded on his upper lip. The smell of sulfur was ripe in the air as he stood up from where he had slept on the floor of the cell. Days had gone by without so much as a single visit from the marshal. Budd worried Greene had given up on finding the truth now he had all of them in his custody.

"Wake up," Budd whispered harshly. "Something ain't right."

Evan woke slowly, followed by the others.

"Is that… sulfur?" asked Dawson, but something changed in his expression. He lunged for Evan. "Get down!"

Budd dove to cover Steven as a hole was blasted into the side of the jailhouse. The force of the explosion sent Budd hurling toward the wall. He hit the brick hard. Pain lanced down his spine as he crumpled to the floor. "You all right?" he asked Steven, who had shaken his head with a droll expression painted on his face.

A cloud of smoke and debris burned their eyes.

"They're breaking free," said Evan as he coughed raggedly.

Salazar, Hector, and Charles led a group of outlaws out of the cell and into the night. They climbed inside a wagon that waited just beyond the walls. A sharp whistle sounded to Budd's left. Blake gestured for them to follow. Budd and the others went in the opposite direction of the bandits, sneaking around the buildings like sly foxes.

Budd pushed open the doors to the stables and spotted Ivory in one stall. He approached his horse slowly and winced at the sight of the matted knots that tangled her mane.

No one had made sure his horse was taken care of in the time he spent locked away. It pained his heart to see her in such a state, but time was of the essence. He took one saddle from the wall and mounted up.

Blake led them out of the city and toward Yosemite Valley. "We have to find the Old Mill," Blake stated firmly. "It's the only way to clear our names."

"How do we know we can trust Pete?" Dawson asked. "I mean, he ain't exactly the most honest person. What was it he told Dotty, anyway?"

"He said there's a ledger at the Old Mill," answered Budd. "Inside are all the details of Ripley Eagleson's plans. It goes into detail about how he acquired Haven Ranch, the attacks on Pratt and Dempcy, and how he ordered his men to burn Black Lake to the ground."

Steven scratched at his jaw and questioned, "How do we prove it's his?"

"Ripley Eagleson's name was branded into the leather. It was a gift from his sister, Beatrice. One of his most prized possessions. I reckon we'll be able to use it against him," said

Budd. "But none of it will mean anything if we can't get Beatrice to come forward."

"Do you think she'll turn on her brother?"

Budd nodded. "From what Pete said, the two of them constantly argued about Eagleson's crimes. If we offer her protection, I'd wager she'll come forward." And he believed that with all his being. There was something to be said about a woman's convictions.

If Beatrice was brave enough to stand up to Ripley Eagleson, then he believed she was brave enough to help get justice for the victims of the Blood Eagle Gang.

But there was a harsh reality that Budd Mansfield faced at that moment.

He had become the very thing he had hated for years— the thing he hunted for over a decade. Budd Mansfield had become an outlaw.

The End

Would you consider leaving a review on Amazon? It would be appreciated.

More westerns are in the works...